AFÉ AND THE CANDLE

Afé and the Candle

Short Stories
by

ANDERS M. SVENNING

Adelaide Books
New York / Lisbon
2021

AFÉ AND THE CANDLE

Short Stories

By Anders M. Svenning

Published by Adelaide Books, New York / Lisbon
adelaidebooks.org

Editor-in-Chief
Stevan V. Nikolic

For any information, please address Adelaide Books
at info@adelaidebooks.org

or write to:

Adelaide Books
244 Fifth Ave. Suite D27
New York, NY, 10001

ISBN: 978-1-954351-42-4

Printed in the United States of America

Contents

We Are Inmate #881129

The verdant grounds of Ellas, that is Greece, undulated on either side of the automobile, which had been on the road for seven hours, and which had in its seats two individuals, friends one could call them, on their way to reconnoiter with Anesto, an acquaintance who had been residing in Albania for the past four years in a small cottage not far from the Ellas border. Anesto, the short and brown individual, had taken up Albanian residence for two reasons. One: his fascist inclinations; and two: his business, one could well call an illegality, and in Albania nobody so much considered illegalities illegalities and that was all right by he. In all actuality, Anesto was not really an acquaintance of the two riding north and west towards the Ellas-Albania border as much as he was a vessel, or exactitude enabling what one may well call escape, and what another may well call suicide. To those two, driving in the small, manual transmission automobile north and west, the two made little difference, and had in their fundaments little difference outside of the peculiar and requisite confines necessary for an escape and the senescence requisite to exact a suicide, and the same applied for Anesto, who was, as far as those two were concerned, a beneficiary.

The planes rolled and unrolled on either side of the automobile, which tinkered and tankered along the railless roads of the mountain, and exacted perilous exchanges minute by minute nearing closer the Albanian border, and the danger was not so much in the precipices, which lined the roads, but more so in the eventual and linear track he who was driving the automobile found himself following, towards an illustrious and finite life. He who was driving was not so different than the bounded seemingness of the environment, which was alive one could well see, and which was, much like the foreboding individual, inquisitive and inquiring the seemingness of that jubilance, making it oasis and reciprocal in its fundaments, which were the fundaments of man in his introduction and a complete Babylon.

The tinsel panels of the automobile's cheap pieces—the vibratory dashboard, the jarred, manual windows, and the radio rattling on what people stated was at hand—brought the passenger into reverie and thirty minutes following out of reverie to the radio host talking about the polices, people, and infrastructure of Ellas in its importance.

"No that's not right," said Zanzios. "That's not why people are leaving."

The radio host continued his soliloquy, which Zanzios named nonsense, and which Zanzios followed with the remark: "Scarcity, Thanasi. Scarcity is the reason they are leaving. Not this and that which sounds sexy. War, hunger. They have their places, but it is the scarcity in the home that is driving people out."

Thanasi had had the rising principle of fascism in his loins for many years, and they had started to rise into his mind with readiness still young in life, and he had written proscriptions, which saw no eager hands, and had written poetry on romance and utopia and dystopia and had come to the fructuous decision there was no big difference outside of the taste of wine and the weight of bread, and that was all right because he had an idea.

Zanzios said, "Material this, ground that. It makes a difference in the blood, Thanasi, and that's it. It changes the molecules."

Thanasi had not spoken of his idea to Zanzios, who was the closest of friends, let alone anybody in relative circles of Ioannina or his mother. He had, leaving the town embosomed in northwestern Ellas, considered the notion of relaying his idea to Zanzios and decided, once near Karies, to withhold his judgement. In all, the idea would be exacted, and it would not include Zanzios, and that was the plan in the very beginning in its conception, and Thanasi would stick to the origins of fruition. Anesto was expecting them, and that was the matter. In Albania, a malleable element conducive to the former of the two motivations, escape, was of importance, and little else besides the grasses and stone cliffs were evident in the mind of Thanasi.

They had entered Karies and exited the town, and then were within kilometers of Kalpaki with its seeming stratum, and then Doliana found itself in the hospitality of two perturbed transients, who were to apprehend nourishment in the form of water, pistachios, and pretzels, and the two were once again in the subterfuge of the interweaving roads, which not interwove themselves with roads, but which were more so fabricated in the embedded topography of that country since the contrivance of viridian and verity.

"What say you?" said Zanzios. "Does the land of Albania have in its borders two consequential happenings this evening?"

"Zanzios, the evening happens much like those who are residing in it, and, yes, Zanzios, Albania will be a battlefield of zealousness and fire in under five hours. Worry you not."

"I'm glad and for no other reason than the scarcity I had been speaking of. It concerns me dearly."

"Me, too."

"What thinks you regarding Anesto and motivation? Will the schmo breach the evening?"

"I think he will join us in our conflagration."

"Very good, Thanasi. I am gladdened by this inevitability. Thanasi, I have had an idea."

"What it is?"

"I have had an idea for a book I will write and it regards œconomics and in an anatomical sense, that is the systems within systems in biology as representative of isolationist œconomics, et cetera, et cetera."

"It sounds precocious." Thanasi had held his own notion of movement to his own and that would stay the case until his removal.

It was a quite organism, of which Thanasi and Zanzios were a part, in Ioannina—all the members of which were writers and seeming, in their headiness, which was not too far separated from wistfulness, and some had apprehended that which was, too, scarce, called popularity, an organism, of which neither Thanasi nor Zanzios were a part, and one of which Anesto was quite provincial.

Anesto had written on botany and chemistry and his books sold little. His change from Ellas to Albania and his transparency did not make him uneducated. He was capable in botanics and in chemistry and well capable at that. One could tell in his caked skin that he resided many hours enlaced with soils and minerals. One could smell it on his person and it was not unlikeable. Neither Thanasi nor Zanzois had seen Anesto in what was now nearing five years. He had left for Albania, that is Anesto had left for Albania, five years prior the pernicious north and westward travels by Thanasi and Zanzios, and had sent a letter to the former delineating address, phone number, and many a peculiarity regarding a child, illegalities, or supposed illegalities, establishments, and other items of likeness both dark and imminent.

"I am thinking if Anesto has written any more works," said Zanzios. "His writings were always interesting."

"Indeed, they were and are if he has continued with the pursuit."

"If he were to make it his foremost occupation he would do well and better than expected, I dare state."

"Anesto has always had a way of action contrary to his appearance."

"He looks to me a worthy and well-composed individual and acts as so."

"Anesto is a dirty and smelly mother fucking idiot."

"Don't say that about Anesto. He has a head one may call lofty, but not idiotic."

"Anesto acts contrary to his appearance is all I am saying. He once, in Peloponnesos, had attained a peculiar fame in dispensing grapes to the locals—he was well respected; don't get me wrong, Zanzios, and the people liked him very much—but he had, and I saw this with my own sight, a pistol tucked into his belt. The pistol was hanging out and the shirt was folded in behind the pistol. I had to tuck the shirt around the pistol so the locals didn't begin to ask questions, not that they would. It isn't the war, Zanzios, and people don't carry pistols around today without a pinch of suspicion."

"One cannot make judgment on a man by appearance. So, there was a pistol in his belt and people saw it. He was dispensing grapes, Thanasi. That is philanthropic."

"It is of no importance, but the pistol is a sign of suspicion, aggressivity, and this. It isn't that I am judging him, but the pistol was a superfluity."

"It may have been."

"Anesto had saved a girl from asphyxiation. He and I were in a café in Ioannina. The café was empty save she, who was asphyxiating, and ourselves, and Anesto, without a hint of hesitation, rose and performed the Heimlich manœuver on the girl, and you know what, she was dressed in scrubs, a nurse from the hospital south of the café out to lunch on that peculiar day, when Anesto saved her from sure death. What thinks you in that regard, Zanzios? Is not Anesto a hypocrite?"

"Not in the least." Zanzios had been looking outward towards the mountain and the sheer façade, on the bottom of which the small automobile kept on in contiguity. "Don't talk bad about Anesto. It upsets me."

"I'm not talking bad about Anesto. I am only relaying some anecdotes."

"Very well. Speak of it no more."

Thanasi did as Zanzios had requested, and spoke not of Anesto in any regard, ill or well, for some hours until nearer the Albanian town, in which he in question, Anesto, lived, the ride having four hours remaining, and, while bucolic, it were rather dismal in the sense the unwinding and humanistic conceptions and the naturalistic undulations feigned and resurfaced within shine stretches in mind.

Thanasi did not tell Zanzios of the time Anesto had received advanced arithmetic aid from an æsthetic, who had been in the street when Anesto was attempting to balance a ledger of legitimate goods he had been selling to farmers, the items—threshes, barrels, and the like—all the while wearing a business suit; neither did he tell Zanzios of the New Year's Eve party of some odd years prior when Anesto had broken into a bedroom being used for a heinous act and cut the man's neck, finishing his life dressed as a cock, but Thanasi was affectated by a number of solutions and questioned if it had all really happened. It was all very estranged.

Guardrails appeared and disappeared within seconds of one another, and in those seconds in lack of guardrails the car lined the precipice with precariousness, leaving not once its track though tentative in its mechanics and passengers, taunting and fescennine; neither spoke, and both, in simultaneity, remarked on the immaculate nocturne, which had descended in themselves, a definitive breakage in amber and zenith and accruing between the two an unspoken deprecation, and one which was not optic, and which was not sensible, but rather more so a dactylic disparagement, equivocal, in between them, and gallant and indelible. The chroma of the skies having transmuted, Thanasi said, "The day has waned. How fairs you?"

"I fair well. I am thinking of Roxanna."

"How has she been?"

"How should I know? I have not seen her in months, six months or thereabouts."

"Where has she gone? Has she told you where she has gone?"

"Yes, she has and no, she has not. She has mentioned her aunt's house in the north, she has said, vague, and I feel as if there is foul play at work in regards to our loyalties."

"That is a shame."

"Indeed."

"Do you feel you will ever see her again?"

"I care not. I only want this obfuscation removed in entirety."

"It will pass as all good things do."

"Good? What is good about longing? What is good about lonesomeness?"

"Longing and lonesomeness are good in that they carry you with them even when you no longer carry them with you."

"It makes sense and it does not make sense."

"Much like everything in the universe."

"It is pernicious, but it does have a certainty in its synchronicity."

Thanasi said, "It is not synergistic. It is an idea that is sovereign and vast."

"I understand."

The notion of Roxanna spurred notions, in subsequence, in Thanasi's collinear mind—Holstein cattle versus sheep in terms of rural œconomics, Zanzios's resilience, materials versus synthetic composites in terms of fabrics for clothing, the reproductive system, metropolises, and the evening in terms of sleep not so much in regards to the act of slumber but in terms of with whom he would have in his bed next to him—and Thanasi, by a miasmic thermal of reverie, had surface in the forefront of his mind, which now was not only collinear, but also sovereign as well as vast, his immediate girlfriend named Lou Lou.

He ignored the seeming face of the girl in his vision as an automobile traveling in the opposite direction approached. It caused Thanasi to manœuver the car out of the way quite close to the precipice and closer than he knew. With verity, he propelled forward the automobile, the corporeal mountain open once more.

Zanzios was not dozing, as he was thirty minutes prior the exchange regarding Roxanna. He was wakeful and attentive. His sclera refracted light from the headlights, in their fractal ways, into Thanasi's own eyes when he looked at Zanzios out of the corner of his own eye. He looked well. One could not state otherwise—and there was something close to dysphoria in his appearance, not in his eyes but in the way his hair was swept to the side and in the way his lips drooped and in the way his arm was rested on the door panel, relaxed and amplified and ready. It was of no concern. It did not upset Thanasi. Thanasi just noticed this small character in his acquaintance's countenance and liked it as one of the last memorandum images of his acquaintance and one he would take with him.

The idea he had formulated was the matter and Thanasi was to exact the idea with flawlessness. He liked this, too. The final three months in Ellas were of importance. Nobody was to like that Thanasi was gone. He liked this, also, and tucked it away in his cacheé of mysteriousness, which one may well call prescience in Ellas, and which would change into a dissociative tendency upon his arrival at his destination, which was west and far more west than he knew.

Ellas kept him in Ellas for two reasons, one of which had already been solved. That one was his kindred mind. The other reason was relevant in so far as the journey to Albania and was the consideration of monetary holdings. Within thirty days, the latter consideration would be apprehended and monetary holdings would be in impoverishment's stead. That Thanasi, Zanzios, and Anesto were to cohabitate and triangulate was, by no means, an hegemonic dejectedness. It was an incubation of precociousness, and Thanasi liked this, as well. He cared not where Zanzios and Anesto arrived neither did he care how they arrived at their predestination; this was what he told himself as he drove along the pipe thin roads towards Albania in an attempt to withstand the efficacy, which had descended in him the terms of finality and enigma.

The soldier in flight, no, not flight he told himself; he had jumped and was inserting his blade into the δεξιά end, that is right hand side, of the enemy foe's neck, the soldier's wrist lithe and gamine, looking not at his compatriot, not in the least, but that which was before him, the buttocks in sight and garrulous, the viewer a viewer of the posterior of his cranium—an effacement of priori currency, not contemporary, not modernistic, not even naturalistic, but paranormal and perturbed, and the question asked which illuminated the desultory eyes of Thanasi along with the image of the soldier, But was he vain? Thanasi made observation after observation regarding the unmovable iconoclast, the lackadaisical wrist, the fluidic hair, which was well manicured and cascading yet, and the buttocks and their volume and shadows, and the feet, the battlefield underneath him, the shoulder and the death in the compatriot's face, and decided without much hesitation that he was not vain and that he was a worthy administrate of unworthiness and of fabrication and of nascence, a decision which made Thanasi happy and with a mirthful boldness not separate from ostentation. He took his mind from battlefields of former epochs to sex.

The type of sex in question, however, was that of the two polarities and not the act of the two ensconced as one, out of which came three. In the soldier's stead, Thanasi's first girlfriend had arrived. The girl, who was named Stephani, had been a quite and seeming girl, and one could not call her daft though she spoke when nobody was speaking to her and spoke in those times nonsensical until Thanasi came to the decision to excise the quite and seeming girl from the day to day pursuits in entirety and with no remorse; for she was crazy, and everybody liked it when she was not in company.

The couch, the rug, the lampshades, and the window curtains all the same color, a mellow orange, had assumed a constancy in that room, which had held both he and she, Thanasi and Stephani, on the evening Thanasi commenced in the conversation, which would enlighten Stephani of their termination and her estrangedness, something of which, Thanasi had told her, she may or may not have known given her laconic ignorance and disagreeability. She snorted and threw back her head and snorted again and was snarky, and Thanasi had patience for neither her apprehensiveness nor her antics and told her she must, if she had not in this discussion, realize she was an harlot of her own accord.

She replied, "I have not realized I am anything of the sort. Tell me how you think I am as so and articulate when you tell me how I am so indolent."

To which, Thanasi replied with fidelity, "Thou has not ear nor soul to apprehend the sublime notion," patronizing and solemn and high.

It had been in the apartment with the uniform color that Thanasi had made the decision to start writing, and it was in the apartment with the uniform color that Thanasi decided also to relinquish superfluities—furniture, girls, clothing of peculiar typologies, foodstuffs, and electricity—and using enough only to survive and to incubate. It was then Thanasi made the decision, though not noted in the forefront of his mind, that he would escape the confines of ordinated homeliness. The foundational strata had been shifted, and passageways into brachial lives had become manifest.

The notion was well known by Thanasi as he drove down the mountain road towards Albania. It could not have been more prevalent. It was so pedantic and cognizant. The three months, which were to unfurl before he, who was more than a preemptory omen—he was quite the omniandre—were to unfurl with quickness and without a kink in their fancy. Thanasi well knew this and could feel it in the posterior of his head, where the notion to skidattle had been visited and revisited many a time, and where the pejorative node was bequeathed by alabaster wanton, an axis of memory and retrocognition; and the island of Andros was in mind; and the Murænidæ with their needle fine teeth and their basil tones were perceived upon sight and were eloped in the clusters of coral off the coasts of Andros, the island not small but not large, an avaricious chequer, delinquent and multicolored. Viscous soils, over which Thanasi manœvered his hands; the hydrogenous sediment, which was of the affectation of the saltine seawater; the biogenous sediment and its progenitor origins; the terrigenous sediment, a demarcated and terrestrial derivation—all, by tidal fluidity, had Thanasi, while retaining his air in his lungs, at the mouth of a cavernous orifice in a cluster of coral, and he perceived the Murænidæ, both it and he motionless, it with its salient lustre and Thanasi with his receptivity, Thanasi glancing only for a second to see the specimen, which was twelve inches in thickness, writhe and discombobulate into the piquancy of desire, transmogrifying and oscillating as an hypnogogic glimpse into Elysia and into the performative visions of he, who was now driving north and west, beside an acquaintance, beside himself, and enraptured.

Zanzios was awoken by a dipped section in the road. "How much longer until we reach the border?"

"One hour to the border, and then one more hour to Anesto's house."

"Very good."

"I would tend to agree."

"I have a joke."

"Humor me."

"This guy has been falling into the mother fucker for four hours. He is just falling and falling—"

"I feel I have heard this joke before."

"Okay, here is another joke."

"Humor me."

"The mother fucker is walking throughout his dominion. He comes to a guy hitting Gehenna, and says to the guy, 'You had better let up for the good of us both.' The guy says nothing. He's hitting Gehenna. The mother fucker says, 'You like what you have become?' The guy who is hitting Gehenna says nothing in return, and the mother fucker walks further into his dominion and comes along this guy and another guy hitting the arch. The mother fucker says, 'You two had better let off before baby gets not so pretty.' The two guys say nothing and continue hitting the arch. 'You are better off ending this asshole now for the both of us,' says the mother fucker. The two do not reply and the mother fucker goes further into his dominion and comes into contact with a guy eating triple cheeseburger after triple cheeseburger after triple cheeseburger. The mother fucker says, 'You need to let up, guy, eating triple cheeseburgers. Know that. It would be better for the two of us.' The guy eating triple cheeseburger after triple cheeseburger after triple cheeseburger is sitting on a bench and stops eating his triple cheeseburger and turns to the mother fucker and says, 'My grandfather lived to see ninety.' The mother fucker says, 'Oh yeah? How'd he do that?' The guy eating triple cheeseburger after triple cheeseburger after triple cheeseburger looks into the mother fucker's eyes and says, 'Because he minded his fucking business.'"

"Zanzios, you are brilliant."

"This is happening, Thanasi. This asshole is relevant."

"Zanzios, to hell with you."

"Don't say that. First, you were talking ill of Anesto and now you are condemning my mind and soul. Don't say that, Thanasi."

"You are his dominion."

"Drive the car to the border well and don't expedite my house."

"I am so Levantant."

"I am thirsty. Is there any water remaining?"

"There is no water remaining. You and I have drinked it all."

"You are a thirsty one. Are you always this thirsty?"

"You don't have to lie to yourself either, Zanzios."

"I would like a drink of the tea you brewed last year."

"It was a good tea."

"It was a mother fucker."

"For some, it may be of matter of course."

"What was in the tea anyway, Thanasi? Remind me. It was a long, scientific name of a type, with which I am not familiar."

"Two parts rooibos, to start, and then two parts sarsaparilla, and then three parts Argyreia nervosa, or, as the far easterners refer it, Adhoguda."

"You collected these parts from the fairy ring, is it?"

"You need not be stark. It was an apothecary, north of Ioannina where I bought the ingredients, the rooibos, the sarsaparilla, and the seed, all the same."

"You contrived it of your own accord, or otherwise the loquacious muse?"

"I heard of the tea by a small circle in Ioannina."

"So, you imbibed our water with rooibos, sarsaparilla, and what was it called?"

"—Argyreia nervosa, or as the far easterners refer it, Adhoguda."

"—and gave it to camaraderie and expected no repercussions?"

"I experienced repercussions, Zanzios. They were not appreciated nor were they pleasant."

"Oh? Are you determined in stating they occurred in yours and my own actuality, or in the trenches of paranoia."

Thanasi said, "The former, Zanzios, and, yes, with determination. Tania and I had drinked the tea one evening, and she initiated the course of thought regarding the induction of one in creating a licentious triangularity."

"Oh? The suggestion did not meet to your acceptability?"

"You don't have to lie to yourself, Zanzios. I have a cache of morality and a conscience, which works in conjunction with the former. That is more than one could say of most males in our nation today."

"Per happenstance, I agree."

"That would be fine."

"Have you read the fictive piece Anesto wrote a couple of years ago?"

"I have. The piece regarding photosynthesis and deciduous wood in some context or another. Yes, I have."

"I'd be very happy if Anesto wrote another fictive piece. I enjoyed it quite a bit. I even conceived something on my own as a result of that short narrative."

The road straightened out into what Thanasi perceived as the stretch of road leading up to the bridge, that is Kakavia Bridge, and the border in between Ellas and Albania. He saw he was correct. The bridge was becoming clear in vision, with its sparse and desultory lighting. One could not call it ugly, or grotesque, demarcated, yes, but forlorn to the point of an hinderance, or questionability, no, not to two individuals, who had been on the mountainous roads through the north and west quadrant of Ellas, and who were showing their first suggestions of peculiarities.

"Anesto's characters shit all over each other. That's Anesto and Thessalonians in entirety. They can get away with it and people call it literature."

The town they entered twenty minutes into the Albanian country was degraded in its structures and its infrastructure—the roads were incomplete and undulating and were made of loose soil—and the town, which was partial in its absolution, was not much different from the Ellas towns, in their scoop houses and in their epigone stratification, luculent and appreciable.

The town of Gjirokastër, the town in which Anesto lived, was forty minutes north and west still, further into the topography, which did not differ in the least from the Ellas mountain ranges. It was a contiguity that made the two separate and sovereign. The continuousness was not a mere diathesis of height and circumferential cues; neither was it a contiguity of the isosceles and tenebrous terrain. It was an impression one got and one made upon the eye and the ear and the nose and even the chest in its reciprocate expressiveness, the mountain being the mountain, the hypnœsis being the hypnœsis.

"Call his work what you want," Zanzios said. "It is thought-provoking."

"Thessalonians have a way of piquant ideas."

"It seems to be the case. It is the same as with he who Anesto had brought to Ioannina years ago from his area in the northeast." Zanzios busied his hands with his shirt strings at his collar. "He had a head on him."

"Indeed."

"What could have happened to him?"

"If one were to open up his head there would be nothing inside."

"He was a daffy. What was he called?"

"We call him acrylonitrile butadiene styrene."

"The devil."

"*O Plastikos.*"

It was in the former of his two years with Tania when Thanasi had produced the most work. He wrote on œconomical systems concerning this and the familial organism affected by that, all in the context of regressive socio-œconomics one may well call remedial œconomics, if one were to look and examine the finite and infinitesimal workable parts of the systematic recapitulation of monies and also value systems. It had elevated in Thanasi a peculiar inclination, one which had three prerequisites, which were as follows: (1) Six strawberry frosted donuts; (2) An empty day, with no substantial appointments as obstacles; and (3) Hungry people. He made a statement once when he was in the streets of Ioannina, giving out the donuts to people, and a girl, who was not a girl by the agedness of her, had asked, or rather suggested they rendezvous in the park at four o'clock for a hot date, which Thanasi did not keep, and which was not of substantiality; and then twice with the wayward bitches and tramps, following the rapid descension of a strawberry frosted donut. The pursuit held fast for twenty days until Thanasi decided he needed to start making money from his literature before commencing in the action and application of his infamous theories. He would walk and dispense of the strawberry frosted donuts and, at most, sixty minutes later, would arrive back at his apartment and make the notion he made to himself each afternoon following such a pursuit, the same notion he made and verbalized in the automobile, kilometers into the Albanian country, "Now I'm not living a lie."

Zanzios said, "What?"

"I'm not going to carp, Zanzios."

"You were not one to carp in the beginning when I met you and you are not one to carp today. Now I'm not living a lie. I know that. If inspiration were contagious—"

It had been following the two parts rooibos, two parts sarsaparilla, and three parts Argyreia nervosa, or as the far easterners refer it, Adhoguda tea when Tania had suggested the licentious triangularity Thanasi had mentioned to Zanzios back within Ellas borders she had wanted to take place between he, Thanasi and she, Tania, and a third person, who went by the name of Duck, and who was, as Thanasi had placed, really a cow, and not for the weight of him—the weight was not too substantial—but rather for the amount of leather, which clothed Duck, and which left Thanasi incredulous and in entirety. Tania was still influenced by the two parts rooibos, two parts sarsaparilla, and three parts Argyreia nervosa, or as the far easterners refer it, Adhoguda tea—Thanasi liked how she had voiced her opinions and desires, but it had become an aberration—and, sitting in the titular points of the geometry, Tania had voiced this desire, too, the desire, in which Duck was to take part in έρος, which was becoming μέρος. The words came from Tania's mouth, and Duck knew she was going to say what she had said, Thanasi could see quite with clarity. He had, of course, replied in the dissent as per the demarcation of Duck and his telegraphed and virulent tendencies, a reply, to which Duck responded Duck do for Thanasi's girl what Thanasi's girl cannot do for herself and to let do what Thanasi cannot do for Thanasi's girl let Duck do for Thanasi; Thanasi was not expecting the response, nor was he expecting to be having this tripartite exchange in the beginning. He was quite ready to distribute strawberry frosted donuts and had them with him at the time of the exchange, and, when the fulmination exited the mouth of Duck, Thanasi removed one strawberry frosted donut and assaulted the leather-bound individual with it, throwing it like the discus and making a wish it would stay on his Cyrano de Bergerac nose like a schwa.

He had taken Tania by the elbow and led her back outside into the Ellas heat and back to their apartment, where they had had the fatalistic reciprocity, which had become a constancy in Thanasi-girl cavorts. "You said you wanted Duck with us?" Thanasi had said. "Tania, that's nasty."

"There is nothing nasty about comprehending intimacy."

"That is not intimacy. That is nasty."

"Oh? You like intimacy. What is the definition of intimacy, Thanasi? Tell me."

"—And the high mysteries to unfold."

In the automobile, the cloth upholstery of the driver's seat was becoming bad in its shabbiness. It was becoming more and more noticeable to Thanasi as they grew nearer and nearer the town, in which Anesto lived. It was not putrid nor was it a discomfort, but it was a constant, which Thanasi was quite in readiness to disregard. The automobile had not any problematic instances over the past five years, nothing of too much gravity, and it was steadfast in its dependability in the travels north and west, and well-acknowledged by Thanasi, surreptitious.

"And we are that much nearer," said Zanzios.

"Indeed."

"You have driven well. I have not had an exchange with the death."

"I'd rather have an exchange with beef stroganoff."

"In Ioannina, I need to get some things."

"Know what you need to get and get them."

"I don't like why I'm getting them, but I am going to have to get them and there is no eluding it."

"For whom are you getting these things?"

"You like her. It's that girl I met from the automotive depot, the girl who is having a shit exchange with something called maternity."

"Yes, that girl is attractive."

"I remember seeing her and looking at her face, and then I remember looking down and looking at her feet, and I liked she noticed it, and I liked her feet. I can tell by somebody's feet who they are—it's a thing I have—and looking at her feet it occurred to me she was going to have a shit exchange with maternity; and, now, ten months later, she is having a group of people over her apartment for a celebration."

"That is appreciable, Zanzios. It seems to me she has become a convivial acquaintance."

"She is a limber and feminine female."

The windshield, which separated the outside of the automobile and the inside of the automobile, was, in its parallelogram invisibility, all Thanasi needed to pervade in himself an appreciation not only for the girl from the automotive depot but also for her descendant, who, Thanasi could well fathom not only as a pressurized notion in the belly and mind of the maternal, but as a pernicious inclusion to Ellas and Ellas comedy.

The Ellas comedy was transferring to an Ellas dysconnectivity, that is to Thanasi, in the diasporic ideologies, which not made valid the decisions of the Ellas people but made valid the accidents of the Ellas people, who were consuming themselves, and who were attriting their beneficence in servility—a sulfuric acid comprised of saprophytes, which would enumerate Thanasi and the bel'ōrəsHən foundations, all to make miniscule and molecularize the notion Thanasi had been having for many a second and many a breath bounding headlong into their destination, beating his chest and breathing, I have arisen, I have arrived, and I have extolled, because I killed myself better than you, liking he was at last, liking he was to retain, and not because he was hardscrabble, but because he was the didactic macron.

Fractals of soups and porous and yeasty dawns and evenings, which enveloped Thanasi had sent him abound, by the inertia of the idea he had had and of its own accord, into the land in the west called America and called New York City. Thanasi had become a commodity and a precious conciliator. In two years' time, he found himself in Riker's Island, performing that which had become a commodity, conciliation—a conversation, on the day of his release, and with a young man named George.

"—An idiot and bullfrog, Redding and Ellington, respectively."

Thanasi had taken on a bit of an American accent. It was not to his knowing, but if he were to return to Ellas following this misfortunate bout with American law, an action, which would not occur, the people of Ioannina would notice the accent and tease him about it, and it would become a joke throughout the town for the duration. Ioannina was not to have Thanasi in its borders, however. Not again would Thanasi slumber in the warm nights of Ellas. He had, on the river across the Manhattan skyline, a place to live—an apartment, which housed a girl named Na Na, who was also from Europe, and who had extended an invitation that Thanasi stay in her apartment, because she was in a possessive grasp on the prisoner and because he was innocent.

"I was never one for the blues," said George, who was sitting at a table inside the small common area, and who was bald but for the sides and back of his head. He was not old. One could see the youth in his face, which was flawless and void of wrinkles. The bald head was the only indication of a criminalistic inclination, a noticeable attribute in the man, who did not like the person, who noticed the rather telegraphed attribute. "That Elton John, though. I will tell you this. He likes his line of work."

"As do I, George."

"Next time, don't fuck up."

"I pleaded not guilty."

"You never committed a crime, Thanasi."

"I like Elton John."

"I like crime."

"Guy? I will tell you what."

"You're out today, though. There's something to say about that."

"It's too bad Norm and I got close."

"The bastard."

"He shouldn't have fucked with that slap happy."

"That nigger wanted to kill him the second Norm walked into Riker's Island."

"Norm should have cracked him over his shit."

George said, "They should retire his number."

"Inmate #881129."

"They recycle numbers. Know that. They must recycle numbers. It's the only way they can stay zero-sum."

The morning Thanasi met with his associate, who incorporated him into the line of work, which brought him to Riker's Island two years following, a white T-shirt and khakis had been assumed, and he was rather pococturante in the way he introduced himself to his associate, who was named Thompson, and, too, in the way he viewed his surroundings, the people, and the architecture, all of which were commonalities but for the small visual cues that made them a continual phantasm. He had walked into the coffee shop, in search for the parameters and the objectives of this inquiry, which had been extended by an individual a month prior in the small smoke bar blocks down from Thanasi's apartment near the shore. It was not so much a smoke bar, in the conventional perceptions of a bar—that is, a bar and a bouncer and lights and disk jockey—and it was not what one would call public, either. It, the smoke bar, called Gill and Burt's, was a small basement, beneath a bar, a conventional bar, that is, which sold beer and liquor in legality, and which liked the business downstairs, as per the near double patron traffic it endeared. Thanasi did not frequent Gill and Burt's. He met the connection there and that was the last time he visited the small, delinquent establishment. He had gotten a phone number, called the phone number, and, seven days later, walked into the coffee shop, where he would meet Thompson and start working as a lifter. The coffee shop, too, was small. The patrons were quite separate from Gill and Burt's. Here they wore clothes, which looked like a psychedelic experience. Those in Gill and Burt's wore clothes, which looked of the dominion of God Hades.

She has her T-shirt. We have nothing to worry about. The papaya, who was ordering a coffee and cinnamon roll, was losing Thanasi's attention as he began again to listen to Thompson, who was talking of nothing at all of that which was at hand. Thompson had gotten some stack last night. Thompson had gotten his ass last night. Thompson had gotten his butt in the right side of the road and had picked it up to a trot. Thompson had gotten his, oh yes, and you are looking for a job. You want to be a lifter. You want to make paper money. Of, course. Of, course. Thanasi, is it? I can do that. There's no question about it. We will even lend you a computer, which you will use for the work, and you will get training in the program et cetera, et cetera. Of course, we hire you because we don't want to get caught. We don't want to be the culprit. We don't want to be the lifter. That's your job. Isn't it, Thanasi? There's no need to sign your name on anything. We don't need your blood or semen. All we need is for you to lift the names and the numbers, and meet us every first Tuesday at — and hand us over the compact disk, which you will exchange for, oh, how does seven hundred and fifty d—. No, how about twelve hundred dollars sound? It's not hard. It's not even crime, Thanasi. You only have to recapitulate the why and the, in this case, who;

and then, we can call this dance the end all and be all, and we can hightail it out of here and never have to come back to this flower child WC again. Do we have a deal, or do we have the veal? Good. I am overjoyed. I will see you on the first Tuesday of next month and somebody will get in contact with you this evening regarding your electronics and training in the software. Have a good evening, lifter—and that was the harangue, which Thompson had made in that coffee shop and the harangue, which was the initiating point of Thanasi's three years in prison, a time, which would begin a fortnight over four hundred days following the agreement, and about one thousand days following his immigration into New York City, America, the land of slopportunity.

The apartment where he lived was not Thanasi's, however. It was the apartment of Elina, his first girl in the stigmapple. She had invited him on the first night they had been together, and Thanasi had stayed and had been staying with Elina for what was nearing twelve months. They ate well and ate together, many times at small cafés in the evening times, which were piquant, and which whetted the appetite of Thanasi for more knickerbocker exchanges and experiences. The exchange with Thompson had been one, which was rather particular. It was not knickerbocker as he perceived knickerbocker, but rather in a swashbuckling sense and as a desultory glance towards a wayward accommodation and metropolitan orderliness. Thanasi had, however, executed his idea. It was done with a flawlessness that could not be distinguished from destiny, not until the late months of his third year in New York City, when the headstrong took a dive into the brackish waters of adjudication.

Lifting names had become easy. The trainer who had trained Thanasi in the software was likeable. The organization for which Thanasi worked was uncorrupt as far as he could see.

The notion of good business and incorruptibility had held fast in mind until the evening of his run in with the American law and his first night in an institution, with walls and wire and spite. He had been seeing the people of New York different when he had grown famous amongst his small people, that is, the market in which he worked. Elina had become meditative. He liked that she did not know his line of work. She was beginning to show signs, however, of questionability, in the way she shook her head in dissent while Thanasi was working at no peculiar thing and in the way she constricted her pupils when she inquired on his work and how he got his money to take her to restaurants and buy her scarfs and shoes and lingerie. Thanasi glanced at her while she was sitting outside on the balcony and made the same notion as when she and Thanasi were outside at their most visited café. There is nothing going on in that head. She is meditative and there is nothing going on in that head. Meditate and think of nothing. It makes me funny. The first time he had this idea it made him funny. The second time he had the idea it made him funnier; and the third time he had the idea it made him single. He did not mind so much. He had much money from lifting names and that was all he needed to sustain. He picked up a place further towards the shore and the apartment was furnished with a few disparaging pieces, the armoire and the night stands and the armchair—all of which stayed in the apartment and were used with a wantonness, which was not ignorant but more so bucolic, a distant hold on the trenchant, penitence and penchants.

His words, which he told Elina upon their final exchange, were becoming a considerable regular. He spoke not of the other, with whom he was speaking, but of himself and attributed his own feelings toward his own person to the other, with whom he was speaking, in this case, Elina, and with a simplistic, "Thou art worthy," a jocular and supercilious trochaic, which was not at all the matter.

The connection, to whom Thanasi gave his disk of names and numbers every first Tuesday of the month, had, on one meeting, told Thanasi of a small kink in the chain of networking and in the organization, for which they both worked, a sort of intrusiveness on the part of a small network, which worked in opposition to their objective, and which was a detective organization hired to extinguish certain criminalistic circles, one of which ordained for extinguishment was their own circle—a quick mention not to lift names with the letter A in the third place and not to lift names with more than three P's in the name in its entirety and not to lift names with the number of consonants in between seven and ten was relayed to Thanasi, who made a note on his hand—because, "Assholes are getting syphilic," said the connection, who was getting mad, one could well see in his facial expressions and in the scarlet elevating up his neck on either side, with incredulity.

"Would you murder a man?" said Thanasi.

"You're a murder a man, you son of a bitch. Be safe and be wary in the names you lift," said the connection, and he returned to his drink.

Thanasi had left the small rendezvous, thinking if he would feel the capability ever in his remaining years. He had not felt anything, to his knowledge, close to the capability of murder, and he did not need to feel that capability. He liked being a composed individual and not crazy, which, he knew, many people, with whom he dealt, were and without hesitancy. He made his names in two categories, (1) Those able to be lifted, that is, those with letters besides the letter A in the third place, names with three or less P's in the name in its entirety, and names with under seven consonants and over ten consonants in one category, and (2) All the names, which fell into the classification of hot, as donned by the connection, that is all names with A in the third place, all names with more than three P's in the name in its entirety, and all names with between seven and ten consonants in the second category—and proceeded to lift names, one by one, finding the appropriate names, addresses, phone numbers, cell phone, house phone, and work phone numbers, social security numbers, foreign passports, credit card and debit card numbers and the pin numbers for each of the types of cards, even bank account numbers and safety deposit box codes and professional codes, used in the workplace—all information, all names, and all identities were lifted, and Thanasi was popular not only amongst his circles, but also in the faux-space, in between the real and the surreal, the natural and the supernatural, and the man and the spirit.

In the weekend prior the first Tuesday of that tenuous month of names, Thanasi found a girl at a local bar and brought her home to his apartment, where they entrenched themselves in one another and made sex. It was the last exchange, in a gregarious way, Thanasi was to have with a female over the next three years. She had said, "Look for me next weekend," musing she would not see him in the next weekend and sounding, she knew, of sticks, tempered and blackened as tinder, and she was out the door, a representation of termination in the otherwise appreciable and lucrative pursuit, on which Thanasi had been with cadence, while within the American border and while within the New York City limits.

The Tuesday had arrived. Thanasi had gone to the rendezvous with the compact disk in his front jacket pocket and had entered the small club, redoubtable. He had ordered a drink and had approached the connection and was in the process of handing over the compact disk, for his two thousand dollars—he had gotten a raise in his commission—and, handing over the compact disk, a man and a woman asked him to come outside, into the autumnal evening, where Thanasi was swung on his foot into the wall and made captive, and he was then brought into a black sports utility vehicle, unmarked and ominous; the jail further eastward would have a patron this evening it did not have in any evenings prior, that was Thanasi, who had learned upon his court hearing that he was guilty of identity fraud and a slew of other charges and he was sentenced five years in prison with parole, next defendant please. Thanasi liked the judge for his lack of professional demeanor, and Thanasi liked that Riker's Island was to have a denizen by the name of Thanasi Eiouiannis, with vehemence—because what else was he to do? Was he to have a conscience, now, after it had removed itself from his faculties? No, in a conscience's stead, Thanasi would see three years of bread and watery noodles and meat, he would see the death of Norm, that is Inmate #881129, and he would get released on good behavior, superseded by a conversation with George at the table inside the small common area.

"White bread."

"Garbage."

"Black pepper."

"Garbage."

"The Belgian Congo."

"Garbage."

"The pitchfork."

"Garbage."

"One can get a lot of use out of the pitchfork, Thanasi."

"I got hit by lifting names not hay."

"Maybe, you would have been a better farmer."

"Struggling and retarded? Artistry would have been a better knowledge domain."

"You can't lift names with a pitchfork."

"Not yet."

"They are meant for usability."

"So are paddles."

"They are meant to thrust quick into unexpected or difficult situations."

"So are paddles."

"The devil doesn't use a paddle. He uses a pitchfork, and he has been in likeness with success, people say."

"He's square."

"You like smoking, Thanasi. I remember you said that. Get a smoke after leaving this prison. Think about what a pitchfork is good for and what is square, really."

"I don't smoke, George. You must be thinking of the conversation we had about Gill and Burt's, the smoke bar. I don't smoke. I only went there for lack of reason."

George said, "I don't wheeze anymore. I came in here wheezing like an alligator in the Florida Everglades. I was quite confrontational."

Thanasi said, "It's good you breathe with ease."

"I'll breathe easier when I'm out of here and with my people."

"I'm out of here and going to Na Na's. You remember I mentioned her some time ago. She's a resourceful girl. One of my first connections in New York was Na Na."

"She may be waiting outside for you now."

"Give us a call when you're out of here. Wait, I'll get a paper and pencil and write down our number." Thanasi got out of his seat, in which he had been sitting for two hours, and one in which he had been waiting with fervency for the reverberant, telemetronic phonics to give him the sign, "Inmate #8—, pack up your bed roll and come to the front pod door for release," at which point he would pack his bed roll and give George his frivolous belongings, perishables, of course, from potato chips to under arm antiperspirant, and take not one glance at his bed, his bunk, where he spent many a night, not sleepless and not nocturnal, but sustaining a certain homeostatic, which was similar to the gulf stream. It took him to a centre of transience, not a transience of the actuality, in which he lived then, but a transience in heroglobal navigation and temporal recognition, iconoclast and superordinated. He had been in gravitation towards this orbiting maleficent for upwards of thirty years, and the centrifugal hands were beginning to remove bounds not ornamented in this prison, or place, or time, but bounds, which had always been there, and which had always constrained the perturbed and affronted Elinai. The ticks and scratches and hematoma were not ticks and scratches and hematoma arrived or attributed to the corporeal barrage, but of the constituted imprints of many a foot and of many an epoch, conglomerated into he, Thanasi, voracious and oscillating into incorrigible tints of metalloids and cytoplasm, invisible and of affectation. The pending release prisoner went into his cell and wrote down the phone number on a piece of paper with the pencil he had and had been using for the past three years. He did not write much, not with this pencil, and the few instances he did write a small notion—they were small sentences or phrases written out of context and out of semblance—the small notion found its way onto the bunk frame, where a few nondescript ideas had been written, but none of which were of consequence. Somebody may read Thanasi's script and think of their woebegone mother's hair in their hometown of Lincoln, Nebraska, or somebody may read Thanasi's script and think of their education on pollination and how the plumage of birds were incorporated in flight, or somebody may read Thanasi's script and think of callused feet in their adolescence, or somebody may read Thanasi's script and think of the creases in their childhood jacket's sleeves or the creases in their childhood playground's concrete or the creases in their childhood reacquaintance with their elder brother, in the oak benches of the nature reserve, with the Santorum and the Lepidoptera. Thanasi brought over to George the sheet of paper, on which had been written the phone number, and he handed him the sheet of paper, which George deposited into his front pocket.

"No problem," Thanasi said.

"I didn't thank you yet."

"Today, you go to the supermarket and the café and the deli and they hand you your sausage and coffee and cheese, and they thank you. You don't even have to thank them. The grocer and barista and delicatessen thank you. They thank you for giving you yours."

"That's something, isn't it?"

"And then, you sit and cut your soppressata, or abruzzese and you drink your coffee and you munch on your cheese, and the real question that dawns on your mind is, who is the mouse and who is the pussy?"

"I—"

"It was a hypothetical question."

"You'd like—"

"Ever since the turn of the century, or even the nineteen-eighties, wood has seemed lighter, hasn't it? It used to be when I touched a table made of wood, or a bowl made of wood, I was touching a table and bowl made of wood from trees. Wood is made in a factory, or in a Petri dish somewheres in Lower Manhattan. They have at the peak of the building the Petri dishes, and they make the formulæ, and, as the wood descends, it becomes more wooden until it reaches the bottom floor, or the loading dock, where it is filed out and into trucks, to be distributed all over the United States of America."

"Oh, yeah? What do you make of that?"

"Shit, George. Different shit."

"And then, we can all sit around and eat shit as a family," George said.

"That may be liked by your fam. It has to do with your decisions, George. We got George, the wise ass, over here. George, the fucking wise ass, here."

"People make bad decisions."

"That's all I'm saying."

"Then we really are beneath the devil's tits."

"I have too many soups. I'm going to get a couple and bring them over here and we'll eat the soup, and you can have what's remaining." Thanasi, once more, had arisen from the table in the small common area and went to his cell, where he took out from underneath his bunk two soups, and then he went back to the table in the small common area, where George was waiting, and where Thanasi was to have his final exchange with George and with the judicial system in entirety. He approached the table, and George turned to Thanasi, and Thanasi tossed the soup onto George's chest. "Thou art worthy that thou hast no more that this thy present lot," Thanasi had said, possessing the soup, and, opening it, he turned to George with his moderate head and told him to enjoy his fucking soup, because that was all a man was to know in Riker's Island.

To see one's walls and to see one's holding pins was one aspect of captivity Thanasi had begun to not enjoy, but appreciate, and not in an œconomical regard, but in a gratified way, as per its evidence and its candidness. Thanasi, in the town of Ioannina, Ellas, had been snagged. He had been snagged, countless instances—caught on the shirt collar by Ioannina girls; left wanton to saunter the streets of Ioannina; washed and drunken in the late evening times in the small house, where he and his expanding family lived; to pick up and to drop off small packages of this and that to acquaintances and exchanging laundered shirts with those, who, too, were a part of that Ioannina circle—so many instances, in fact, that he started to begin to believe he were the snag and the others, the other items and people, the Ioannina girls and the streets and the drunken bathing and the exchanges, small packages and laundered shirts, were getting snagged on him, Thanasi a thorn, Thanasi a peg, Thanasi a hook, Thanasi a knob. It was then when the idea had struck him, that he was to move west and farther west than the west he perceived as the west, because the walls and the holding pins in Ioannina, Ellas were not optical. They were not auditory nor were they able to be felt, nor smelled nor tasted, and the walls and the holding pins, here, were quite optical and quite auditory. The reverberation sustained throughout the evenings, night after night, when an inmate cleared his throat or when an inmate cried or screamed. It stayed with an inmate even after he had been released, tucked into his loins as a transparent identity, which surfaced only when people inquired, and which squelched only when the rattling chains and metallic security portcullises were lowered and utilized at closing hour in the streets of New York and one could taste captivity. Thanasi ate his soup until it was low, and then he wadded up the wrapper and sauntered over to the garbage can to throw it away, in subtlety. Approaching the table in the small common area, Thanasi exchanged places with George. George arose and walked over to the garbage can and did the same as Thanasi had done, with more gusto and with more apprehensiveness than Thanasi had in throwing away his wrapper, but nobody looked and nobody cared and nobody was able to understand this were their attempt to steal something, a fructuous smidgen of humanity from the place, into which they had descended inmates, degenerated miscreants, confined spirits in New York City and confined to dress in the prison and, too, as subjects of depravity.

George walked over to the table in the small common area and sat down in his seat. "Thanasi, you're out of here in sixty minutes. It's like I can make it happen."

"Make it happen fast."

"You would like this thought I've been having."

Thanasi said, "Oh?"

"One can follow all the presidents back to the year of independence, that is 1776."

"Right."

"Women got the right to vote in, what? Nineteen-twenty something."

"Okay."

"Blacks got the right to vote in the nineteen-sixties."

"Really?"

"Oh, yes. Now, what about the canine. Have they not a right to vote?"

"I am going to fight for you," Thanasi said. "I am going to fight for you. That is the most sensible thing you have said since your entrance into Riker's Island. I am going to fight for you."

"I am no person to fight for."

"Really?"

"I am nothing to fight for, Thanasi."

"If you want to be something to fight for, kill yourself."

"It would be that easy," said George. "But, how much money would you give me to do the thing?"

"Twenty million United States dollars."

"I'll take it."

"Do you want the periodic payment or the lump sum?"

"Hit me with the lump sum."

"I never got that."

"The funds?"

"No, the decision to take the lump sum over the periodic payment. I am incredulous, thinking about it. What fool would take the lump sum, George?—I don't want the latter ten million dollars."

"I don't like the notion of a handful of electronic money being uploaded into my bank account every month. Hit me with the lump sum. I don't have a drug dependency problem. If I did, I wouldn't be around to see U.S. dollar ten million and one."

"Don't say you wouldn't," said Thanasi. Thanasi noticed the porous, white mouth on the wall had addressed him. In some respects, he liked the floundering and spurious abandon.

Afé and the Candle

Alexandria was in a crisis. The denizenry bequoth war. It was to escalate with order for economic decency. Those were social treatises. The integrity of the Ptolemaic scholars had declined. All was nothing. Medicinal theories had become bilateral. Interpolations were fabric. The cotton fields nicked the hands of harvesters. Musical competitions were judged relentless converse to talent. Gaap reconstructed Babylonian importance.

Cracked walls of businesses and buildings, by poverty-stricken workers, were schpackled back to presentability. The heights, with which these lot were dealing, were forty meters on an average. The free-standing persons were withal privileges of the politico regime of before Christ Mesopotamia. Damascus and Antioch, too, had this chaste symmetry. Determination was not a scarce item. All who sounded at the Helio ouroboros possessed some uncanny drive, which vacuumed their spiritual intentions inward to an equal and opposite place of warmth. The solar residence was a reciprocate. The real names of misogynistic families had been lost. The rescripted symbols arrived through bodies of alchemlial affectation. Laboratories functioned in full and carried into the metaphysical. Sculptures and paintings of cranberry and avocado pastes and planchettes of the Ptolemy VIII Physchon were forged. The hats of elevate, zygotic veritables were just beginning to see the effects of the inaccuratate knowledge.

Elemental practices were a majority and dissociative preference. Demarcated houses held blasphemous executions of men and ghosts. Witch doctors patronized the melody of divine ardor to perish. Their determination shook the ground. Critics scorned the truth. Auditoria ringed creedo for valueless notes. Underqualified musicians plucked and strummed for kings and queens. Sectionated *logos* cordoned off the desire to sing the appropriate song. Tethered *agapi* slung candor and smelt passages. The arts and psychologic thunder bled through into amalgamated tail ends. The fractured sobriety of former Egypt fruated absurdity prone. Flight via substance did not yield in the slightest.

An accident amounted. Quality of clothes and food, art and validation, and leisure and happiness reached a discrepancy. There was no longer, in the city of Alexandria, justice for the rigmarole people. The differentiation in money hiked the apprehensive grasp on sanity in the great Mesopotamian city of arts and science; the metalloid currencies of former genarti exchanged itself with currency of papyri. The sudden and dangerous, twice-fold wealth of the Empire removed all stability. It was not pun that lent aid to that animus; one tempted that cacheé as an ultimatum, or penchant rebuke. Staccati banks arose and in their offices were tables of gold coin, silver, and copper, and there was a confessionless banker writing papyrus bank notes by hand to procure money. In the discovery of banking, the Mesopotamian nation and even the globe were committing euthanasia, and the scholars of the widespread library system were not guiltless. The uprisal of rebellion prime leaked into the streets of Alexandria. Their patience did expire. For the decency of the nobility, they died. The death, however, was not one of bodaic ends. It was an early admittance into afterlife. An imperial counterattack was in motion. The kings and scholars promised themselves immortal beings. The untouchable seat was being pinched and usurped. The intellectual laundered their own redoubled wealth. Papyrus held not weight in mælstromic citizens. Serapeum, the gathering place of the scholars, maintained erect by stolid workmanship. Individuals stopped their fight. The Serapeum, vandalized by its own constructers, demolished longevity flush. All wanted see plight burn.

Captivation symbologized by business, men fought. Not a lick of textiles found themselves in common hands. All burned and it burned well in popular opinion. It seemed now the low race had an immediate twist. Those of a higher chaste were beaten on a green sight. The furious lust of jaded men remained in their impoverished homes when scholars were expelled Greece-ward for further lone research. The manner, by which Ptolemaic intellectuals dominated the society and seceded from the libraries, were individualistic. They redacted philosophy, moot, while cities were destroyed in tandem with pristine and sarcastic lies. It was cheap entertainment, but there were to be some cheaper in Greece. Shot, the track of mysterious men were in question. They fled with their valued lives to teach boys grammatics. Some took their wives in the country. The cowls women wore in Alexandria donned themselves not around the heads of Greek betrothed women. They bound around their bodies dresses of domestic cotton and were bareheaded for the lack of heat and for the religion. Across the Mediterranean Sea intellectuals and women mourned the destruction and rampaging of their home city. The tricks, which were played on the teachers of wit, circled round. Those who left were teachers of all Greeks, barbarians, and glory voided. Their fear and lacked containment was an iron warning.

The Library of Alexandria retained scholars of few number. The majority studied from home. The library networked scholars. The spirit of the Library of Alexandria was quite alive. It was said that its determined structure were conscious. Those were the fulminating theories of the clerics. No importance what they did write, the Library of Alexandria could not be sustained for the social, political, and economic problems of course and for the syntheses and reworkings of one's own originalities based upon fabricated *ethos*. The fluidine nutrients spread away from the public cisterns. Emulate scholars as if by want took suggestion by watery strings. Spickets were pumped for good fun. The city and its resources were exhaustible. People forgot that the Earth, too, washed money but with washboards and soap, grain mills and point blacksmiths. The diasporic crisis was a pine bucket being thrown out the open door and diminished seeming, metropolitan likeness.

48 BC, the Roman emperor, emperor Cæsar decided to sack the city of Alexandria. He crossed, on galleons, the Ionian Sea and stopped first in Venice for a restock of resources. Once within sight of the mouth of the Nile River, he heard over the high winds the disparate call of pagan rites. The emperor was different from the Egyptian lot of recent years for the plunder. It was not a slow change into monotheist psychology neither a sovereign difference in between the Roman Empire and that of the Ptolemy dynasty. The Roman Empire were to sure put the reign of dynastic hypocrisy to end, they, with confidence, between bites of fish, and of equally chaste society, felt. The supple hairs of the denizens stood up at the sight of the Roman navy.

The battle started with quickness. The Nile River were possessed by the foreign navy. The city-wide devastation with rapidity got uncontrollable. The generals embarked their own ships and, with success, attempted to cut off and keep severed the Romans and their seafaring communication with their Pope in Rome. The adorned walls of the Library of Alexandria were once more beginning to find themselves in flames.

Emperor Cæsar was a conceited, official man. At the slightest wisp of defeat he grew irritated and cruel. All, however, was done systematic. The capture of the wharf and the plunder of the immediate areas desulted prior versions of order. Thus, the vast area of Roman Empire proper. Alexandria and Egypt were different. The climate raised homeostasis. The temperature altered metabolism. Emperor Cæsar was angry.

The Egyptian fleet circled the motionless Roman navy. The tawdry ships kept the Roman navy at bay. Firearms began their rapport. The most obvious fact dawned on the Emperor. The battle was quite finished. Out of spite, instruments were flung and shattered, on the land and on the ships, which were boarded. The polytheistic Gods were in increasing pain by the diminution done to their temples and so were the priests, citizens, and scholars in licking agony for the knowledge their temples, homes, and libraries scorched the night horizon. The fury autosuggested writhing hybrids in this thigaboo. These daytime visions opened pathways of darkness. All heard that instilled silence. It was now a part of the men, women, and children. After midday, Emperor Cæsar gave the order to ignite his own ships. The docks, too, caught, viper fast. Grain storage were on the coast.

The area surrounding the burning ships and docks were a ghetto. The impoverished, skilled workers of the city resided in these areas and remained in posits spiritual that the flames did not reach their homes. There was no defense against the Roman arbiter. The ghettos spread far south until the Library of Alexandria discrept the difference in between ghetto and the outskirts of the noble residence. The roads, which led to the Library of Alexandria, whetted the eyes of foot soldiers for the towering business of research, and the roads by mourning families stayed a mineral difference in between the pillagers and the Alexandrian æsthetic. The scholarly hypocrisy far outweighed that of the Romans. It were a material hypocrisy. It was tacit and counterclockwise. The two-way psychology of Egyptian scholars and socio-political leaders made black white. Their coffee grinds stayed clean.

The future was the broken as those barbarians, who left for Greece, felt they may have been in monies. Mouseion, the main centre for research, hosted visitors with scholarly intentions, but it was not a physical berth lent to the researchers. The means of transportation taken by hysterical scholars still used wheels. There, the canvass blocked their head from the sun. Like the elder years, the individual work done by scholars and professors and their originalities were done from their own homes and behind closed eyelids and in underground laboratories and garages for chemists and engineers. The wheels turned, but they were in the minds of men. They brought them closer to the Library of Alexandria. The inquiries of those in scholarship were to ride on the wings of mystical fauna and to herd them. The desire for professors was a difficult one. It granted the membership of those on scholarship as unwarranted. The feet of the lion carried to Cleopatra 200,000 scrolls and nearer the Library of Alexandria. The consistent sun and the striking façade of the Library spoke relayance to scholars proper. Eucalyptus were aflame. Along the coast of the Nile, they scented the heated Egyptian air. The Library of Alexandria was a complete conflagration. The eyes of children swelled shut. The hearts of women shut. The fists of men closed and were thrown. Anywhere one turned armada assaulted honor. One million writ crackled under blazing fire.

To take the riots of 1967 Lakeland, Florida into consideration made unruly Arthur Ioannou. The dinner by the loud word had become silent. Everybody was wordless many seconds more. The prolix run on of words rather ended. One in dark blouse, the Greek man at the table, again got verbose and was untoward. He was speaking English. Matter of fact, the party were rowdy.

"I do not know what they're fighting," said man in dark blouse.

"Show me the money." Arthur Ioannou uncorked a fourth bottle of wine and said his vows. Arthur Ioannou, too, was Greek but identified as an American made man and was right. The civil rights movement was at a loss. There was no doubt in his mind. The Molotov cocktail had been thrown into the store front window. The States was in disarray by the universal riots. The make shift bomb, into the grocery store, which was white owned was hurled and the Floridian disorder begun, and the humidified, sub-tropic air was the much denser for it. It was an explorative idea for Arthur Ioannou to progene. The conversation at the dinner table was as open as the grocery store front, and men and women in 1967 entered the plunderable store of food and of wine as did the foursome in the present-day dining room pursue controversial reciprocity. The American couple at the pine wood table and the Greek couple were handsome, fearless, and not hindered by pro se wit. Arthur once more took the reins.

"—And that was indiscriminate violence." The words of the American made man were tenuous but not considerate. As the host of the party, he liked to get raucous (the apartment was his home, one which was purchased recent) and was in complete contentedness speaking loud, using profanity, and speaking inappropriate words of a conservative type when the topic of social movement, political science, and the Florida riots arrived in conversation. Not to mention the 1967 riots of Riviera Beach, Florida when tear gas was used on the debauched crowd of African American men and women and the national guard was brought in to quell the civil disobedience and those of West Palm Beach, Florida when four hundred bodies were swelled in the streets of the since uncontrollable beach town, forty six getting incarcerated with a total of $350,000 of damage; in the deflated, economic weight of the mid-twentieth century it was a considerable sum; the Tampa riots in Florida during the 1967 sanguine disingenuousness 11-14 June, sweltering hot and muggy peninsular climate with one hundred arrested, two million dollars total worth of damage, and with one Black man and one police officer killed.

Arthur Ioannou affiliated himself with some nascent crowds in his youth but nothing to the effect of rioters. With even American men of colored skin he associated. They smoked dope, an aspect of American life to which Arthur Ioannou was not in favor and parted ways for a blither lot. To retain the youthful famousness was a desire. He fell in with an engineering society. The recollectable instances from the stretch of time he spent with civil disobedient crowds, those who broke the laws and social graces of contemporary society and order sequestered themselves in the forefront of his fondest memories. The host told nobody of this likeness and he, himself, could not have known for the conservative residence he touted. The philosophical sequence of youthful instances, which were recollectable with the probability of conversational intent, did talk go that way, narrowed his poetic feet and kept him skinny and healthy to the effect of diction. He had quite good breath control. "My father instilled conformist ideals in me," said Arthur Ioannou, a forward man of chance reservation. He made an affectative self-assessment and postulated the lysteric, tropospheric constipulation of opening the fifth, rose, and walked to countertop.

Back at the table, he sat and twisted off the cap and glinted the possibility of bringing Venezuela into the discussion. The South American nation had had a visitor who was Arthur Ioannou when it was in order, lax, and more tribalistic. As a child, the American visited the jungle nation of Venezuela with his father while his mother were on sabbatical. The stick, ceramic vase, and flute displayed the spectral tradition of the country from the table under the window. Through the crystal and the undefined reflection of one's face one might see the Athenian metropolis unfurl. Many ideas for decorative surfaced in the middle-aged man and his regards upon entrance into the small, two-bedroom apartment. Time elapsed turned brief in their decision to acquire that apartment. There seemed to be a meter, which was unspoken between he and his wife, who sat at the head of the table and listened to Greek man in dark blouse speak about his physical work.

"—But I call it cerebral. Really, I do not know—"

Arthur Ioannou succumbed to the effects of the drink. He was taken into a recollection of his father in the Amazon rainforest with Ornithuræ on his shoulders and a breast. The button-down shirt had been punctured, like immunized skin. The immobilized image replayed its virile, brassine moment by the reconstruction of the tropical memoranda.

"—What they're trying. Is life in America the precious I feel it is? I may be mad but I did like the documentary I saw regarding the industrial, oil mining biz and its projection through the decade."

"Our company works oil mining machine manufacture."

"It is a very hands on field of work I imagine, sir."

"It is for the mechanics." Arthur Ioannou glanced at the flute. "It's a very elastic project they tout."

"Elastics are a good start."

In order to encrypt their self-reliant software, the machinery, engines for cars, elevator programs, and their corporate businesses employed the company, for which Arthur Ioannou worked. The host of the party was at the point he might encrypt a software program *vis a vis* manual encryption and etch *The Son of Man* into a pane of glass.

"It is a new company and their doing splendid. Everything is getting more and more hands off today."

Man in dark blouse said, "You hear more and more of people fearful of losing their jobs to artificial intelligence."

Arthur Ioannou said, "It's a valid fear."

"It is a question of the actual professions and their longevity rather than employment. By 2,500 we will all be still and programs will deactivate themselves."

"That's inception," said Greek woman.

"That's murder," said man in dark blouse. "But I can't go that far. Androids only have a degree of consciousness."

"That's my job in there, my man. It's to make computers smart. I'll keep a keen eye on keeping them commonplace."

"Lest the wars with AI begin for our modern enjoyment," said the Greek man.

The dinner patrons embossed each other with characteristic expressions and old familiarities, which were in all of reality new; for the freshness of the camaraderie, all found a comfort in one another epoch old. The craned, Martian summer lent berth and what irony were to access human fair haven! To the global population, over the bowed course of time, embosomed children to withstand the ingestion and the allocation of foreign bodies and the mountains of Peloponnesos and the Americas alike were no different in primal effect. All in question reconnoitered with the planes of life and finality but received its wisdom different than the other, in stark directions and large ways, as had taken place the Inquisition in the Albigensian peninsula in the same year as the Anglican pilgrimage to the new world.

Tennessean hills resided the Quaker peoples, who still spoke their eighteenth-century accents in their most present generation. The plains surrounding which oasis possessed still their hauntings, by cause of the American Civil War and the Turner's Rebellion; the somatic populace remained conducted by wispy presences, fingers tapping, and anarchy in the hills.

1831, sixty men, women, and children perished in the uprisal of Nat Turner and his rebels. The Belmont plantation saw the worst of the effects. The state, of course, retaliated. This were a natural, humanistic decision. An additional sixty men of the opposite color skin were killed by white statesmen and one hundred more by militia. The physicality were a shared and notty ideal; and it were religious in its pure indiscrimination. The serpent reared its head. The rebellion leader, Nat Turner, did see the serpent in a vision and it bespoke to him he will see the sign, which were to indicate the right time for the slave rebellion. The following week and its solar eclipse suggested time. The last will be the first and the first will be the last. Those were words by which Nat Turner lived, with his heretical practices and fructuous impulsivity. The entire showcase really became theatrical. The execution of white men, women, and children, followed by the state's and militia's retaliation surfaced entertainment. There, exhibited, was universal mirth. Further precautions were taken following the quell of that rebellion. Blacks, enslaved and free, might still convalesce in churches and religious sermons, but a white minister was required to be present. It was a must have, patronizing and principality. The only time was death for spiritual assertion.

Arthur Ioannou knew history. He was aware of points in history like the Nat Turner rebellion and the implemented Jim Crow Laws. His work was quite relevant, and he believed in open legislation. Conservative but modest, he set the record straight. "She travelled in theatre. My first girlfriend were really an idiot."

"I think that's funny," said the wife of Arthur Ioannou.

"She travelled around in theatre and played in productions like *Titus Andronicus* and *Henry VI* where it got bloody. She were all right on stage, but she brought the actress home with her. I cannot say it was a good character trait, especially for a screechy, Elizabethan actress. The plays were really kind of cross." It were a thematic philanthropy that dictated Arthur Ioannou and his words. He recollected the sacks full of hay representing beheaded crania of the Duke of Somerset and the Good Duke Humfrey. If always Arthur Ioannou were immune to such sickness and mirth. The emancipation of impoverished peoples in the productions unfolded into the decapitation of the nobility same as the emancipation of Blacks in America, mid-twentieth century and before, led to the beheading of tutors and students for their attempt to trump the challenge to read. Heads on poles found their way down Southern streets following the Nat Turner rebellion much as they did find their way onto the Elizabethan stage, albeit faux, making *Titus Andronicus* and *Henry VI* and their playwright, William Shakespeare, a prophetical entity. His and all brilliance recurred every single night. The illiteracy which breeded in the enslaved, indentured, and free Black Americans in the nineteenth century affronted the hawk and the tree. Instead, the cormorant envisaged the Black body. Decency disappeared.

The vast purchase of verdure by reconstructionist statesmen housed that coup, the Turner's Rebellion, in 1831 Anno Domini, and everything from then on stayed corporeal. The splintered, oaken theatre was all that was missing. Conscientiousity and much else, too, was in lieu of satisfactory life in nineteenth century America and in America in its present, rapid day, thus the Ioannou and their move to Europe. A quarter of the bottle of whiskey had been drinked. The kitchen made a terse beep. The *pastistio* was about ready to be served. It was a recipe the wife of Arthur Ioannou brought with her from the States with the intention of having friends over.

Arthur Ioannou in secret abhorred his acquaintances in Florida. He perhaps did not even know about his distaste for them. The populace of Florida was overwhelmed by heat and conceit in some instances. Arthur Ioannou was not separate from it. The dense atmosphere clouded judgment. His affiliates could even be good for all he knew, but he in Athens, Greece, thought he was dishonest to himself about it, the acquisition of the home in Athens much too good; he fibbed his way to Greece, a demarcated nation from one of supposed stature. His temporal mind had made an imploration. What it needed in return was a signature. To hear the etched parchment of contractual purchase was all that was in want to berth morale from the intemperate, subtropical climates to one of Mediterranean health. As much as he had told his first girlfriend, who acted in theatre, she was well, he told himself he, too, were in an orderly place to keep his nose clean of trouble, as a drinker and as a man. Arthur Ioannou fancied the Floridian populace as handsome, but untalented. Undeft on its dancing feet, Florida had become for Arthur Ioannou drab and in want of a living public. All was very much Elizabethan in its acrimonious, reclusive summer days. Baby blue turned to mauve and had stricken the wife of Arthur Ioannou, Kaitlyn, who went to take a glance at the *pastistio* in the oven. Florida became to her ephemeral. Kaitlyn desired very much.

"—Are more cordial today. They stay in their own neighborhoods and speak well of people who are good to them. That can only be called basic progress," Arthur Ioannou said. "They are rounder today and not so aggressively composed in their containment," the host said.

"That is an interesting picture you have there," said man in dark blouse, motioning to the picture hanging from the wall.

"That is an inscribed planter shape and used very often in determined software engineering." Arthur Ioannou sighted the sphere within cube. The inradius line was visible. The painting was a beige display of simple geometry. The lines drew across the sphere as diameters, latitudinal and longitudinal, and the cube, which contained the bisectioned sphere, was a slight red for æsthetic taste. To view the painting one way lended its three-dimensional view and adjusting your vision had the inscribed planer shape in two dimensions.

"The inscribed planter shape," Arthur Ioannou was saying, "is an illusion. It is a two-dimensional geometry. The colors bring out its three-dimensional quality, the shades and tones. In an engineer way, especially a software engineer way, it has to be flawed. One cannot say chromatics are included in black and white code writing. The shades and tones of this algorithm are, well, rustic."

Man in dark blouse said, "I am not in the know about high arithmetic and algorithms. Let us just be thankful I am not writing aerospace code. The stylistic shape of that geometry looks good, if artistry is at all involved with writing code or likewise a spoken language. It is a good addition to your home."

"Thank you."

Kaitlyn, the wife of Arthur Ioannou, said, "It would be good to have Allison here."

"Allison prefers being by herself," said Arthur Ioannou. He was tough, but affectionate, toward his daughter. "Allison is in her senior year of high school," Arthur Ioannou said, talking to the guests. "We trust her very much so." He took a sip of whiskey and swallowed hard, then took another, finishing the drink. "Can I pour you some more whiskey, Giorgo?" said Arthur.

"Yes, pour some in my glass, Kirio."

At this point, the bottle of scotch were half full. Both the host and the guest, Arthur Ioannou and Giorgos Evangelou, forked the *pastitsio* into their dry regards. It was thick and senescent. The elevate flavor piqued in Euclidean space, poised, and in the party, which was still rowdy; the women coy and drinking Zinfandel, discussed amongst themselves in quiet voices, around the small pine wood table, their children and their collegiate accomplishments. Above the buffer and by pure drink and intrigue a further height licked the Euclid, superlative flower.

"Where are you headed?" said the man in dark blouse, Giorgo. "You cannot stay in Athens for a month. There is so much to do elsewhere."

"Tomorrow we are going to Ministiraki and then this coming weekend we are going to Mavrovouni for a few days, then Creté, prior our daughter's birthday. She will have fun. She will be with her friends for the night. Kait, I think I'm guilty."

"No, you're not."

"I am guilty, Kait. I'm bashful. I've decided. I'm guilty."

"You're flush."

"Perhaps we shouldn't have left Ally by herself."

"You've been drinking. Don't feel guilty."

"I've never broken a thing in my life. I'd hate to start now with Ally's heart, leaving her at home."

Giorgo, man in dark blouse, said, "She will be safe. Perhaps a riot won't start."

Arthur said, "I am drunk. I'll forget about it."

"I'm smashed," said Giorgo.

"I'm drunk as s—."

"I'm loaded."

"Let us," said the host, "remain in control of ourselves."

"Unlike," the guest, Giorgo, said, "the civil rights movement and the Floridian riots."

Arthur Ioannou said, "Unlike the civil right movement and the Floridian riots."

Giorgo said, "Do you have a history of drinking heavy?"

"History of an unruly type goes back centuries all the way to the Egyptian cities and riots of a dishonest socio-political nature, and what society isn't normative in a garrish—"

Giorgo said, "Perhaps stay your thirst."

"—excrement for the germination of their fields—"

"That's original."

Kaitlyn said, "Stop it."

"Yes, I will stop my useless rambling."

Latitude and longitudinal speed and time, curved in between the two- and three-dimensional circle and spheres of inscribed planter shape on wall, beige but red, and real line relationships; the independence from an indelible Empire; Cæsarian, affine space; the Egyptian fleet; seven-hundred thousand books and scrolls; and the Grecian urn—all descended as the able salts of the good Earth.

The Earth and its circumference had been discovered accurate. It landed straight on the motive subters of all in the room. The Valley of the Kings had been opened. The torches used blew, unlit, by the moved slabs, which enclosed the burial chamber. The gaseous nature of the tomb were unlike any noxious crew. The bones of Kings and their Queens and pet animals got transported out of their respective chambers and brought to laboratories for testing of chemical and magnified type. Scientists and lead excavator, Howard Carter, scrounged the porous, aged workings. Gold leaf palates of scripture, aquamarine necklaces, and silver rings were dated and put into stock houses. Museums then exhibited them. The manifest serpent and canary symbolized the death of lead excavator, Howard Carter. He witnessed the symbol of war first hand. The singular death of he made the death a personal deed. The Kings and Queens of the Valley of Kings were still alive. Their spirits casted over the Sahara Dessert with an iron grasp. They dwelt among the nomadic tribes. High, the crevassed regards of contemporary man awoke, old concepts and foundations schpackled tight shut. The living reparation took place. Damaged carvings repaired their flaws of their own accord. The trite sensation encircled all living creatures in the anteroom.

The cracked features of Giorgo, Greek man in dark blouse, and wife flattened after their brief chortling. No gargantuan yet squeezed those who were dining in discontented spirits. The priests of the Valley of Kings were to not deem halooable a lot so ignoble. The indecision to make kin, however, feigned much like the dense, ærated condition did in the tombs of the Valley of the Kings once they were opened and disparate. Intellect envisaged kindness. *Eros* casted heart. Poetic intent turned to fault lines. The Mouseion then housed the blazes of doubled over men, with ideologies anew and cool breezes.

That the ancient Egyptian research institute, Mouseion, served as a temple for the worshipers of Greco-Egyptian goddess Serapis, which was sculpted as a stone, angular business in the center of that temple, and which flawed the contemporary research institute, for which Arthur worked, as a short-sighted centre for research and corrigible by antediluvian tradition, was uncouth, but the software engineer resided very much so in a pro se religious sphere and it were ingrained in him young in life that the way in which bipartisan, proletariat corps reposed at night atop a stratum of rock was itself religious and disconcerting.

Following their stints in Mavrovouni and Creté, Arthur and wife would visit Vienna. After a one day-one night layover, they would reconnoiter with their daughter. The trip gave Arthur time to contemplate the lacklustre sequence he had written. It was incorrect. The new project blew the lid off of outdated sources for news articles and essays, museum galleries and symphonic orchestras. Information retrieval was to be revolutionized as a result of this project, but the final sequence of writ the software engineer had written was absent of an important, semantic cleft. Arthur had not spoken about this work to people. He was telling Giorgo about the Venezuelan trinkets. They breathed dark colors from the under-window table.

"I must go to the car for something." Giorgo rose, put on his sandals, and went out the front door of the apartment. The door closed, quiet.

The wife of Giorgo said, "He is going to the car for something. We could not come empty handed."

"You could have."

"Of course not," said the wife, and her husband, Giorgo, who was rather drunk, walked back into the apartment with a small barrel of raw barley in his arms. He was wearing one sandal.

"This is for you."

"Oh," Kaitlyn said. "Thank you."

"Thank you," said Arthur. "But where is your other sandal?"

"Where is my other sandal?" said Giorgo, and then he laughed. "Where is my other sandal?"

So, all at dinner went to work searching for the missing sandal of Giorgo Evangelou, searching under book cases and couches, armchairs and glass cases.

"I can attest you walked in here with two sandals," said Arthur.

"This I know."

"Where is your sandal, Giorgo? Did you walk outside with two sandals?"

"I did. It must be outside in the grass."

Arthur said, "I will consider it a form of thanks."

Giorgo said, "We will find it later. Let us sit and enjoy our dinner."

"Of course. More whiskey?"

"Yes."

Arthur handed the bottle of scotch to Giorgo Evangelou, who poured himself a glass. Of all in attendance, none that was brought in was left. The missing sandal was one of elusivity. The foursome was just beginning to get acquainted in full. They were a mutual acquaintance via the aunt of Arthur and compatible. All did what they could to recapture their original chemistry and succeeded. The city glimmered through the open window. Giorgo retained his sanity. A missing sandal was the least of his problems. Arthur was included. Really, the electrical writ, on which he had been working for six months, bothered him. It was a globular conundrum, and he was beginning to feel intimidated by its severe nature. It was of no importance. The party closed. Search for the sandal began once more, outside. Arthur and Giorgo stood in the grass. The street was lit, but dim.

"Arthur, we must find my sandal come Hell and high water."

"People are shoeless around the world, Giorgo. Here's to the night." Arthur finished his whiskey. "Let's go inside, Giorgomou."

They sat around the table, which was cleaned of plates, and they were eating *baklava*. The conversation was about loyalty and the civil disobedient loyalty to survival. "It is a Darwinist thing. It is survival of the fittest. The shattering of store front windows is something else. I'm not sure I agree with such deviance," Arthur was saying. "This is becoming a self-preservation issue."

A quarter bottle rested on the table. Giorgo said to his wife, "Have a drink."

"No, I cannot."

"You're my distinguished guest, Voula," Arthur Ioannou said. "If you want a drink go right ahead."

"We are kith and kin," said Giorgo. "Have a drink."

"I do not think so."

"It will do you no harm."

"I might not for the one in my womb. You're pressuring me."

"That's all right. Have no drink. I am not mad."

"You are mad."

"Napoleon Bonaparte was mad. Henry Ford was mad. Nazi Germany was mad."

"Anyway," said Arthur. "I assure you the context in which I was speaking about the civil right movement is unbiased. There is only room for conjecture. Many academics agree in the discussion and accentuation of disobedience. Liberal professors of economics believe in the legalization of counterfeit money. Those of health sciences believe in choice, unprotected relations and human growth hormones."

The guests walked to their car. Arthur and Kaitlyn Ioannou stood in the grass. They bid adieu. The eucalyptus, too, did sway in the hot wind. The married couple went back inside the apartment. Arthur regarded his work close. It was foremost in his regards for the last hour or so of their company at dinner. No task was easy, with the software engineer. This one proved even more difficult, but it was for a noble cause and was revolutionary. Arthur Ioannou felt reservation at first hearing the details of the project, then he warmed up to the idea of being a philanthrope.

Arthur and Kaitlyn climbed the single flight of stairs to their apartment. On a warm day, one broke a sweat. It was no struggle this night for the well air conditioned and spacious stairwell. Kaitlyn used both her hands to balance herself, climbing the stairs. They reached the front door, which was still unlocked. The open door lent berth to a spacious apartment, but not large to a lavish extent. It was humble and modest. A dining room table, which was not large, stood in the foreground of the apartment. On the right side were the living room with television, couch, and futon. On the left-hand side was the kitchen with a countertop, which let a glimpse of the kitchen through. Otherwise, the body would have to walk around the corner, into the kitchen, off of which corner was the master bedroom. Further into the apartment and corridor was a guest bedroom, or Allison's bedroom if she stayed for a while with them in Athens sometime in the future. It was a probability, which was open, and which made Arthur glad.

The remnants of the scotch whiskey were at the bottom of the fifth, and the bottle was on the dining room table. Arthur sat to polish it off. He poured his drink and drank deep, pressing the hot whiskey with his neck. Kaitlyn sat for a minute and said few words regarding the dress the other woman wore to the dinner and then went inside the master bedroom to change into her nightgown. Arthur glinted off of the idea: saturation point, water vapor. The algorithm, on which he was working, applied to affiliate research institutes around the world nearby impoverished areas and metropolises, and the work was in close relation to three-dimensional printers and information retrieval. The people at his company really might win, if he wrote the algorithm with accuracy, global recognition.

There came a point when the written sequence no longer responded. It was baffling. Derivative after derivative, the solution progressed and got bigger and more substantial until it just stopped. An essential point, which every four and seven derivatives surfaced, was absent. It wasn't there. The plotted geometric points turned up collinear line segments. It was poetic, but scary. The arithmetic was flush. The curvature of the solution became shoddy and porous until there was nothing. It was a self-destructive, euthanasic pattern and seemed alive for many segments until gone, kaput. The hole would be plugged, Arthur Ioannou knew, but he did not know how. He nursed his whiskey and shifted in his seat at the notion of poverty-stricken areas and their seemless education. It seemed too good to be true, let alone a truth, on which he was working. The night and the air coming in through the open window started beading around the brow of Arthur Ioannou. They might even manifest air conditioning units for impoverished families and power them with electricity no want for an outlet. The arithmetic, on which Arthur Ioannou worked, in the daytime hours, during the piquant heat of Athens, Greece, and Mavrovouni and Creté, was to be finished by the time of his arrival back in the United States of America. He had discovered the saturation point; dew formed in the projection software in mock application of the technology, and condensation begun at the sentence marking the foundational math the code no longer responded to as external influence and its eventual end. The machine back in the

United States was already in the process of being constructed. The question was how was its sister machine to be introduced to poverty-stricken areas and what interface was to be used once there, in the research centers on the outskirts of the impoverished neighborhoods and in the metropolises. That were the job of software engineer, Arthur Ioannou, and his team of two. No need for more than a triplet. The others were to check his work, if he even figured it out to begin with. The sequence opened up until it got porous, or popped. It were like the inscribed planter shape were a bubble and ruptured. At that point the literature would either go through or engulf the ghettos in sickness. It was an issue his two partners ran through the applicative mock software upon finish. The spiral opened once more and closed. It did manifest the air conditioning units and literature for the impoverished. This was contemporary science and unbelievable at its source. It rocked the foundation of all the modern sciences. There was nothing anybody could do to stop it.

The bold, printed clothes got received at the front steps of homes in Angola and Pakistan. Household decorative were made and brought to the homes by effortless preference of their owners. Gender relations bridged. Criminal factions bonded. The two thousand years of Mesopotamian war lulled. Infants slept in comfortable bedrooms and their mothers sustained a presentable kitchen. The arts surged with originalities anew. The politicians spoke; the athletes batted cricket balls. The military generals maintained their hunting and shooting clubs for the thrill seekers. Quality of life rose, in general, and, for Arthur Ioannou, life came full circle in unparalleled religiosity. It was his show. He had the reins, and he might even deliver.

There were bold prints of clothes and blankets, which were the material representation a person and their electronic preferentiality procreated *vis a vis* the missing interface. How to access the user and their preferences was an emotional process. It was something around which the software engineer was trying to work. In all effects, the lucky user uploaded their preferences and started their double life until the better of the two took over, and in entirety.

Uploading the information at first began with the decisive action to pick an origin. People, however, as a user, decided a location on an x-y axis as a location of their preference as far as its color, shape, or size. The image was a complete one but was sectioned into parts like a grid used for one just beginning the art of drawing, and then the image changed and the tile of preference changed, and the process went on for a certain amount of images until one got to the cafeteria and decided their food for their lunch break, at which time other, physical tests were undergone. It was very complex and private. By the end of the sequence of tests, the genetic composition of the user was uploaded into the program for reasons of preference and for the budding double life.

The scotch whiskey was finished and Arthur Ioannou contemplated taking a look at his work, but decided he was too drunk. He looked into the master bedroom. Kaitlyn lay asleep in the bed with her sweet body. The night warmed his blood. He felt the closeness of his own desires. She was just inside the bedroom, but, before walking inside the master bedroom, Arthur Ioannou walked out into the dining room and put on his shoes. The ball pein hammer lay on the table underneath the window. It had been borrowed from the neighbor and used to hammer in the painting of the inscribed planter shape not one week prior the housewarming party. The software engineer had made the hammer against the wall with two heavy knocks and the nail was embedded in the wall, as intended. The tapestry he was hanging tomorrow lay rolled up against the cloth couch.

The tapestry and its image was the anatomy of a nymph at a pond. There were Cervidæ and Ornithuræ, and she had her thin hand raised toward the tree, heartbreak grass, Yellow Jessamine, and flower petals, as the imports of material sunlight and as the exports of red, faunal flatulence. The forsaken splendor grinded passages to gravel; and there somebody were in exhibition with the twisted and final flight of damselfly, tranquil and of sources serene, of opalescent vision and of onyx excursions. Arthur rooted around in the grass. He stumbled into the sandal. In was beneath the fig tree. He saw it as a good sign. It was cold and wet. He picked it up and squeezed Hygeia.

Gelsemium incited local paralysis. Arthur Ioannou regarded what it was to be raving mad. The indigenous tribes tested lichen to taste. The budding froth sometimes exited the mouths of men. Convulsions and asphyxia then ensued. The fearless tribes ruled still the plains. To survive the counteraction always meant the men were getting stronger, the herbal treatments for indigenous sicknesses were improving fast, and the Riri spirit were to commune over the course of the night for solace. No nighttime dreams came to Arthur on this sullen night. In fact, it were a nightmare in broad, shining sunlight. A herd of sheep blocked the road.

The roadway unwound the further one got from Athens. The Peloponnesian mountains shone on one side and reflected the rays of the sun. Their brown faces were unlike any other mountain range in their venous momentum. They were used as defenses against foreign armies. The range as defense were effective for the reason their faces were so much so sheer cliffs and the unmovable home of soldiers. Cackling rites were done in the stone crevasses. The first mountain was seen fifty kilometers after leaving Athens with a southward discourse. All was lithe verdure. Those stayed untouched lands.

Arthur Ioannou entered the hallowed land, elated by its monastic openness. The rush of Athenian life aged the gentleman. His software was more so the culprit. He knew this only too well. A hint of fatigue had made itself prevalent recent weeks. To leave for a couple weeks to Mavrovouni and Creté was a very sought for end for Arthur Ioannou. The verdure redoubled once they hit Peloponnesos. There was no stopping until they reached the beach; and then this forsaken herd procured an obstacle.

The city left behind the two maddened itself with a growing populace. Here, on the winded roads of the middle country, there was not a body to obstruct their forward motion. In what sadistic realm does this obstruction procure itself, and for thirty minutes! To sit before this herd of sheep and remain motionless was madness. It spun a web of absence in the head and feet of Arthur Ioannou, who remained stuck in the logistical row. He were to fire off the engine, spark plugs and cylinders combusting, gasoline and pistons pumping, and make his way through the head of sheep, slow as not to expire a lonesome head of sheep in the heat of the impatience he was just starting to exhibit. It seemed the madness carried on outward from the metropolis of Athens into the heartland of Ellas in the form of hoofed Animalia, retarded by collective consciousness. It were only a question of their accumulating on the grasses, upon the nudge to be given by Arthur and his rental car. The herd was to take to motion once more. Arthur Ioannou did not want to play shepherd, but he would if the obstruction remained for very much longer, on the cliff side road. This dog was barking, ape s—, beside their rental car and had been for the past twenty or thirty minutes.

The shepherd dog had, many times, walked through the immobilized herd of sheep, but they did not respond. It seemed the herd was in possession of a paralysis-stricken hand. The local farmer whose sheep this were might be more pissed than Arthur Ioannou imagined. His sheep were assured late for their resurface in their pens. At this point, the farmer and shepherd of a human type, anyway, was waiting for and giving his dog more time. Within three hours, he would begin planning a search operation for the witless herd, which blocked the narrow road southward toward Mavrovouni, and which blocked the Ioannou from their vacation on the beaches. This was a more immediate problem in want of a solution, rather than the software program, on which Arthur was to work once in Mavrovouni at choice hours throughout the week. The dog barked incessant at Arthur's driver's side window. The face used a primordial indiscrimination. If Arthur opened his door he was sure to get mauled, attacked, or even killed by this Canis beast. It wanted blood. It barked loud.

Spittle flew from and dripped from the Canis breed and its gaping mouth. The froth had not begun. There was no sickness in this specimen. The saliva were caused by one reason and one reason alone, Arthur Ioannou and his presence on the lands of former Spartan nobility and as a foreign body on the plains. The dog and its aggression surfaced in software engineer Arthur Ioannou an idea, a shepherd program for his software, which was to work in conjunction with the derivative. The shepherd program was to guide the interface around the porous sections of code and other holes in the written sequence. It seemed to the engineer it could work. First, however, was the accomplishment to get his car through this stagnant herd of sheep. They bleated from their square place, and it was heard in the rental car, amusing but having reached an expiration in its amusement for its tardiness to leave; the idea already having been picked up by the software engineer, the herd was no longer useful.

The blood thirsty dog followed the rental car at its driver's side window when Arthur Ioannou let off the brakes and began rolling toward the immobile sheep.

Kaitlyn roused. "Are you going to go through them?" She had been sleeping.

"I am going to try to," Arthur said. "See if this rabid dog doesn't lose its bricks."

"He looks like a mean one," Kaitlyn said. "For a sheep dog."

"He's mad," said Arthur. "It's time to get through this alkaloid coniine, serious lupis inceptivate." Arthur, for jokes, spoke in a lisp and checked his watch. Kaitlyn had the tattoo. Sylvester the Cat on her glute. It had been an accident at the University. People farked up. Arthur Ioannou was just teasing her to a certain extent. Arthur Ioannou, though, did not like to bother her about such things and was proper. He used the appropriate amount of gaiety, speaking like that to not upset the sotie of Sylvester the Cat. "He's a mad dog," Arthur said. "Let's sandwich!" Arthur Ioannou pressed the gas pedal and nudged his first head of sheep. The shepherd dog was losing its ass. It was miraculous. The sheep began to part. "Notice how he keeps his head on," Arthur said.

Kaitlyn said, "Stay course."

"Crippled head." A head of sheep lay bloodied up in the middle of the road. Arthur and his wife drove up to the herd of sheep when it was already immobilized. The healthy sheep huddled around the injured one. An automobile must have hit the damaged head. It lay bleating on the asphalt. All Arthur wanted to do was reach Mavrovouni and hit a reserve lager.

A twenty by twenty interface, with dining rooms and vases, faces with acne and café-au-lait marks, speced imagination, but that metal-faced dog was the one over whom to prevail first. He barked and blocked the fair road. It was a common fate the strap, in-pocket regards of Arthur Ioannou, software engineer, did not break on failure. He resolved to dye the code. He gassed it and pressed through the guardian dog, a metallic streak through the forsaken splendor of nymph Theophane and Hygeia. The discretion Arthur had used, waiting for the head of sheep to move was a bit excessive, but he was in a peculiar and presumptive state, one in which the elusive sequence of code may have been solved.

Movement were once more achieved. The two by sundown were driving slow through the streets of the town, Mavrovouni. The indium night descended upon their shoulders and suggested a café nearby their hotel as the restaurant to visit. They were close but had been a good thirty kilometers away when Arthur started to get hungry and when Kaitlyn put away in their luggage the snack they were eating. They drove through the solemn beach town of Mavrovouni. Kaitlyn remained patient and in the passenger seat. The software engineer then located the hotel establishment.

"I like the dress," he said.

"It's coming off tonight."

"Oh," said Arthur. "I like it when you're mean."

"I know that."

"Where is the acoustic guitar?" said Arthur. "I know you. You forgot it on purpose." Arthur pulled his hand back inside of the rental car. "Bring your marbles. We may have a hard time getting food. It's midnight." The man and wife were hungry. They chimed their way to the café some thirty meters out from the hotel. Those were small steps and wanted. The deepening waters of Mavrovouni swelled full on their left-hand side. The streetlamp illumined the lone, sandy road. A staircase appeared at the corner of the café and its property. In the apex of the indium night, Chiroptera beat their silk wings. With sonic location, they located flies and fruit. They worked neither with sight, nor did they with momentum. Those were the only fauna capable of true flight. They batted tattered wings and achieved their ærial. They sustained their effortless airborne with calcar and femoral shaft, and tragus and concha. Theirs was the white noise syndrome. They heard nothing, saw nothing. The roost was over yon in hollow trees and their trunks.

"I suppose there is semblance," Kaitlyn said, rightful.

The two had reached the lonesome café. The small sign on the darkened front door window read closed. Arthur opened the door and poked his head inside the unlit dining room. A workman was shifting drinking glasses from one milk crate to another. "Can we eat?" The inquiry received no response for a few seconds longer than expected.

"We are closed," said the employee. "It is midnight."

"We have not eaten. Let us eat. I will tip the kitchen."

"Okay," the employee man said. "Come in. Let us make it quick. I have to get home. I will be the cook and the waiter."

"Thank you," said Arthur, who walked in, held the door open for Kaitlyn, and closed the door. "Thank you."

"I am the cook in normal cases, so it is not a big deal. I will cook well for you. What would you want?"

"I already know what I am having," said Arthur. "What about you, Kaitlyn?"

Arthur ordered a beer and the lamb, and Kaitlyn the octopus hors d'oeuvre. "Excellent," said Arthur. "This beer is good."

A couple, who were hot in argument, entered the café. They sounded English. The cook was in the kitchen and did not come outside upon their boisterous entrance. All had been in order. The couple had not been heard for the clanging noise in the nearby kitchen. It were really tempestuous.

"Why?" said the English girl. "Why her?"

The English man began beating his chest, saying, "I'm a man. I'm a man." There was no telling what made this ninny so much so a miscreant. There were incredible goings on in England, and this sharp-cut man and his girlfriend were not one of them. Arthur gathered they were an item from the, "Why her?" He was able to tell the male had made the mistake of seeing another girl. It were obvious.

Kaitlyn said, "I hope she's all right."

The cook came outside and addressed Arthur and Kaitlyn and told them the food was almost ready, and then he asked the English couple if he could lend help. The Englishman ordered a beer, which was served fast. At least there was understanding. The bartender, or cook was not at all upset.

A third English person came in the café. He said, "Come. They are fighting in the lawn." The first of the English men, who came in the café when Arthur and wife were inside, and who had cheated on his girlfriend exited the café with the beer glass in hand and without paying for the drink. The Englishmen on vacation in Greece were an anarchical type. The British vacationers discriminated only so much. The food, the lamb for Arthur and the octopus hors d'oeuvre, was served. Arthur paid twice as much as the bill read, and they walked the thirty meters, past the Chiroptera flyers, back to the hotel, in the lobby of which Arthur purchased two bottles of water and two bars of chocolate for the mini refrigerator in their hotel room. Kaitlyn began reading her book, Stoker's *Dracula*, and Arthur ate half a chocolate bar and put the remaining candy in the mini refrigerator. He changed into a pair of pajamas and put on a tee-shirt, making the chi maneuver removing his shirt, Kaitlyn rising and stating,

"This book makes me hot."

Arthur said, "You are hot."

At the foot of the king bed, she dropped her dress to expose wax breasts and her thicket and turned round and spread her glutes to show her dark brown butt. She took him into her hot, silken throat, with decant forwardness. Arthur squat on her exuberant posterior. She cried out. Husband and wife went through with that honest intention, the mythological risqué and deictic blood in their own, the ancient formations of adrenaline and neurological structures released in their arterial passageways, good today and gone tomorrow. The two piqued at the Amaranthine plateau and, by the means of sea and foam, they ascended the primal spinal column deux qophs, to Sradhithara place, with spoken mantra, Suffering succotash.

Four thousand kilometers south and west the diamond industry was experiencing a strike, while the blistering jazz of Herbie Hancock and Maceo Parker was played in towns like Jacksonville, Florida and Charleston, South Carolina. One thousand men withstood the need to work. Fifteen hundred men had been fired outright. That which was guilty of appropriating the indelibility of the Earth was the human race. No lonesome man was at fault. Drills shattered the rocky Earth. Over epochs, stones ordinaire manifested as gems. They were excavated from the dense, African mines; the men scoured them for diamonds. Those precious, hidden jewels thrummed. In a trans-Atlantic realm, instrumentation rang out as attempts on reticence. The traditional African had changed into Gaap. They took the ears of white men. Asiatic machinery slammed hard Babylon. All over, they propelled the systematic destruction. Seismic vibrations stayed in the hands of the work men. There were now much fewer men who worked mines. The blades of drills and swords chipped away the thrones of Gods. The foundation of Earthly glory was becoming exhausted and it lended berth to the astral premises of false truths in every God damned person who touched that centre of tranquility. The deities of Earth bode time. All seemed, however, fruitless. One thousand men were out of work. Fifteen hundred still had been sacked, irrevocable. One afore caveat stayed consistent, civil war.

Prismatic spectre opened in their brassine, ultra-lit. Hygeia sat at her high seat atop Olympus and listened to the guttural noises of nymph Theophane on the island of Samos. "How much longer can this go on?" She shifted her gaze to the son of nymph Nephele. Phrixos was riding the gold ram to Colchis, or present-day Georgia. "At least Phrixos is having good transit on the golden ram." She spoke to her father, Asklepios, "He will arrive in good time in Colchis for the sacrifice."

Asklepios said, "He will make it just in time for the change of the seasons, when Hades takes Persephone."

"Yes."

"Hermes' insurmountable greed cannot play in our favor," said Asklepios.

"Hermes willing they will go to copper laden Colchis unmolested."

"Let us hope."

Hygeia said, "At least Hermes spared a ram from the white note."

"He remains steadfast in his theory his is the best rod for Theophane," said Asklepios.

"Your rod is the best rod and will heal Theophane."

"I do agree," Asklepios said.

"Where is Hermes now?" said Hygeia.

Asklepios said, "He toys with his simulations. The theatrics of wooing Persephone back to Olympus is important to him. He rehearses, incessant, for the coming season of spring."

Hygeia rose and traversed the floor to the liquid portcullis. She entered and at will went into the chambers of Hermes. He stood before a phantom rendition of Hades. Persephone sat on the couch beside him. Hermes, dressed in white linen, spoke to Persephone, exclusive. His words were meant for her to hear so that she may heed them and go back to Mount Olympus following the fast approaching winter season.

Hermes said, "You shall rule all that lives and moves." The basso voice, with which Hermes spoke, was unmistakable and commanding. Hygeia listened for many seconds more. The phantasm of Persephone shifted in the shaft of luminescence, beneath which she sat, as it had last year and the year before that year, all the way rearward unto the original seduction of Persephone by Hermes to reenter Olympus as the God she were before she was taken by Hades.

Hygeia spoke, in a lull in the rehearsal. "Hermes," said Hygeia. "You must grant Phrixos good transit to Colchis. He is only a boy and likes you."

Hermes continued with his simulated rehearsal of the retrieval of Persephone. Hades listened, with intensity, at the positive aspects and affirmations given by Hermes should he let Persephone back into Mount Olympus and out of the Underworld for short periods of time.

"Hermes!"

"Thy will shall be done, Hygeia." Hermes said, "I want to show you something. It regards your patron and his wife in quiet Mavrovouni." Hermes spoke to his acolytes and told them to alter the simulation. It showed Arthur Ioannou and his wife in heat. "This is the *ayion*, who tries to hack my simulations. He is enjoying his wife a bit too much for good taste, don't you think? I will grant good transit to the son of nymph Nephele, Phrixos, but I will not grant this *ayion* his repetitive attempts at code."

"You and your simulations," Hygeia said.

"He will not hack my simulations if I say so."

"That may be true; but, Hermes, that code may stop the paradox relations—"

"I will hear no more of it," said Hermes.

"God Zeus may feel differently," Hygeia said, "than your stance on the issue until Phrixos is granted his needs in his traverse through Greece to Colchis."

"We shall see. The golden ram will be sacrificed as always to quell Poseidon," said Hermes.

Hygeia spoke seductive in her gentle contralto. "The uprising in the Underworld may instigate the perpetuation of this feared technology if you do not please Hades. I fear for you he may want the *ayion* to succeed." The God of healing, Hygeia, shifted her gaze to Phrixos riding the golden ram through Greece, which scintillated as an emerald, and which gleamed pre-lit. The Greek landscape twisted constant and abated fatigue. The golden ram had thus far carried Phrixos well. They navigated through the dense, hence, untraveled verdure. The two spoke in interspersed conversation. Many monies had been betted on the punctual arrival of the golden ram to Colchis. Confidence was instilled in young Phrixos. He aged not since their original travels through Babylon and Thessaloniki. The ritualistic repetition of the divine enactments were necessary. The theatrics necessitated themselves in the will of the deities. Those rituals—the traverse through Greece to Colchis upon the golden ram, the killing of the Cyclops in Sicily by Apollo, the capture of nymph Theophane, the seduction of Persephone by Hades, and the murder of Asklepios—kept the unchangeable habits and relevance of the Gods near and of importance. Each year, the typical experiences which had been lived by Gods in the Eocene era were rekindled and experienced in a small, pressurized window of time and money. The consolidated, divine happenings made probable the advancement of science in the human race. Hermes had grown fearful. Hades rejoiced. The incredulous populace of Mount Olympus stood at a divide in the recent years of technological development and were stirred into a contemporary uproar of fleeting differences and threats. Very few outside the ritualistic battles took place and few Gods for the fear of Zeus and his reprimands followed through with their spoken words of violence and their riotous intentions; but some did, in a passive direction, take and deliver small offenses toward since unheard of instances of disrespect, darkness, and volition. For the once more surfaced month, during which Phrixos traversed the Greek landscape upon the golden ram, many Gods were relieved at the inevitable arrival and sacrifice of the steed to quell the insatiable lust of Poseidon for nymph Theophane if only for another year. The seasons were about to change.

The healthy saturation of streams and air with gold flakes told Phrixos all was as it should be. Flawed nonetheless, the comfortable landscape of Greece accepted he and the golden ram again, as it had the preceding year. "We make good time," said Phrixos. He addressed the golden ram, atop which he rode.

The golden ram responded in falsetto. The steed, whose backside were gripped by the young Phrixos, agreed. He had not once failed in his transportation of the young God. The beast and his logic remained, however, unbeknownst to his ultimate fate. Poseidon made sure of it. The golden ram made the young God Phrixos aware of the wolf spirit, which was close by. This was a new development. The journey northward and eastward had not been before this year one which had unfortunate encounters with other beasts of prey. "We must walk careful and slow," said the golden ram in his falsetto voice, "as to not attract the attention of the cannibal."

"I agree," Phrixos said. "But we must make time. Keep good speed. The seasons are said to change within the week."

The ram said, "We will make time." A stick snapped loud on their left. Phrixos and the golden ram turned left to gain sight. No animal of prey seen, they picked up to fast pace. The mountainous region of Thessaloniki just exited the two. The two penetrated the first lands, which were not Greek. Every time the two affiliated rode to Colchis, they ate and lived well. The bright dawns, which, one after another, bequoth elevated psyche of man and beast reached apex in the fern labyrinthine. Upon exit of Thessaloniki and entrance into the first of non-Greek lands the sap of lichen creaked in favor. The air began to smell of chamomile. Olive trees twisted into civil, finite life. At the beginnings of Colchis, the constructions men built began to make themselves quite known. Querns became evident along the banks of the river Phasis and grain mills spun in their blades. The corn fields, systematic, too, began to betray their undeniable wealth of quantity. The unrefined Thessalonikian lands ended abrupt with Šara. Phrixos gripped the coarse wool of the golden ram, riding upon his haunches. Those were typical days under the stars. The yellow orb of the sun bowed and refracted into the eyes of the duo. The redness of the descending sun was agreement. The ram was to be sacrificed on time in Colchis. Zeus had confirmed that control. Variable after variable, Hermes took away seeming threats anew.

The God of land travels and thievery was surprised and, in secret, aghast. So many—too many—new threats made themselves evident to the traveling Phrixos and the golden ram. It were a bad omen insofar as the science of Man and *ayion*. The failure to deliver the golden ram for sacrifice in punctual time for the change of the seasons, Hermes knew, as he sat with Hygeia, facilitating the travels of Phrixos and the golden ram, was tantamount for the maintained order of the Underworld and to withhold the inspiration of the *ayion* in Mavrovouni. The consistent threats Hermes warded off was suggestion enough the *ayion* was making progress, and the tardy sacrifice of the golden ram were to anger Poseidon and enable Hades to let disorder reign throughout his domain in the Underworld and in all things which lived and moved. The technology, which Hermes was so much against for his own relevance, were to be birthed into the Earthy realm if the ram did not sacrifice in time and in money. Also, the will of Hygeia, God of healing, was to be sequestered. The importance of her regards was invaluable to the God of land travel and thievery, Hermes, for his insatiable greed for spoon fed healing and importance atop Mount Olympus and in the Earthy realm of Man and beast. To take the health of nymph Theophane into consideration ignited an unparalleled thirst in Hermes for lustre and its spatiality, the changing of the seasons and its effortless curvature around the spherical contrivance of the great delft Earth. It were a stark fact. The golden ram was one of the stolen sheep of Apollo, but Hermes cared not that it was Apollo's by birthright for its annual undyingness and portent immortality. The only problem for Hermes, who closed the pre-lit vision of Phrixos upon the golden ram, was that the *ayion* in Mavrovouni was a patron of Hygeia and lucky. The God of healing, Hygeia, had decided to take especial care of the son of nymph Nephele, that was Phrixos, while his mother, Theophane, was in captivity on the island of Samos. Hermes said, in his transparent tone, "I am in between two difficult predicaments, Hygeia. You know this, as you know all. I must please many Gods and have limited resources, these my simulations. How can I function, with properness, if they are hacked by Man. You must withstand the requests of that *ayion*."

Hygeia said, "We shall see in the cleanness of the sacrifice of the golden ram and in the effectual healing of nymph Theophane, who, have mercy, still undergoes the relentless tortures of Poseidon as an ewe on that forsaken island in the Aegean Sea. Perhaps I can hold his intellect for a time long enough to grant you developments in your simulations so that his code does not affect your offices, but his is of a human's will. They are unaffected time and time again by Gods." Hygeia rolled her eyes to expose the whites of her sclera. "Besides, I like the way the *ayion* and his wife interact and feel he is doing very well."

"He's borderline immoral."

"I am well aware of them and their intra-pursuits," said Hygeia. Hygeia had a secret, too. She wanted the *ayion* to succeed in his science. Arthur and Kaitlyn finished up their experience; Hygeia walked back through the liquid portcullis, leaving Hermes. She reconnoitered with her father, Asklepios, who sat at his throne. The room were an ovular architecture. Many monies had passed through this chamber. Countless instances brought the Gods together in council. This was the room in which the council took place. Another, Hygeia reflected, was to take place and one regarding her patron *ayion*, Arthur Ioannou. The God of healing took her seat beside her father, Asklepios, who roused from trance. "Another bleak recurrence?" she said.

"They are becoming frequent," said Asklepios.

Hygeia was, of course, asking about the flashback, which occurred to her father when he was embodied as constellation Ophiuchus. The issue was one to bring up at the soonest council. "For a time, I want to supervise the pursuits of nymph Theophane on the island of Samos."

Asklepios said, "Must we delve into such rot."

"It is my responsibility," Hygeia said. "As is her nephew, Phrixos, as rot. Do not speak badly, father."

"You have my apologies. Ask your acolytes to aid you in such a responsibility. Poseidon and his lust for nymph Theophane is becoming unlike what is used to be, flawed, yes, and indecent."

"The pursuits on the island of Samos have only been the indecent you are feeling listening to the anarchy on that isle."

Asklepios said, "Let us call forth nymph Theophane and her wild consort." The eyes of Asklepios still bore the whiteness they had bore when he first escaped his prison on constellation Ophiuchus, and the bowed stratosphere glinted further as he spoke the words which brought forth the ugly, perverse visions which stemmed from the island of Samos, on which nymph Theophane was, constant, subject, to Poseidon's immoral lustre.

The elements and everlasting anger was noticeable in the ewe form of the nymph, as Poseidon in his *xeni* form had her from the back for weeks in subsequency. The stomach of Asklepios turned, with roiled sickness. The outlandish noises emanated. Those sounds were unable of being heard long. The incredulous took place on the island Samos. Like every famed yore of God, the rot was annual. By the turn of the seasons, the golden ram was to be sacrificed and the lust of Poseidon quelled. This summer, however, there was more interference. The simulations of Hermes were subject to tamperings. The Underworld of Hades was threatening in a possible uprising. The threats which encountered the son of nymph Nephele, Phrixos, and the golden ram were three-fold. The lust with which nymph Theophane was met this year, by Poseidon, too, experienced its multiplicity. The bowed stratosphere of Asklepios further wonked away. He winced and was met with visions he had had as constellation Ophiuchus. The endless store of Serpentes was horrid to him. Those were of the worst recurring visions with which he had to deal, and he loathed Zeus for his original murder. Hygeia and her father, Asklepios, further watched the bee hive, which had manifested around the head of the nymph Theophane, as she was in her ewe form, and the humiliation and the wrath. Asklepios took to a specimen Chiroptera, flew down, and biffed heads. No relief reached nymph Theophane. She gazed eastward, while Poseidon had her, out and over the Seven Stadium Channel into Asia Minor, or present-day Turkey. Samos was quite near the historiographical enemies of the Greek Gods, and she did not find even a slight pleasure at being on the island of Samos with Poseidon and her consort. The island of Samos lay only fifteen-hundred kilometers off the coast of Asia Minor and the offenses kept persisting. Asklepios always began to get personal, each year, around the same time, when the orgy was having a pique and getting near its finality. The amplitude carried in an eastward wind the cries of the nymph Theophane, and the Asiatic peoples of present-day Turkey many times hatted the ears of their children and knew, in that original exchange between she, nymph Theophane, and the God Poseidon, volition took place and that the Gods made love. Separate from the precept of the notty exchange—the coarse hair of nymph Theophane, twisted and pulled, came uprooted—the childish fancy she once took in regards to priori worth was emptied by the vacuum that was Poseidon and his lust for the nymph Theophane and her angular facial characters, the high, dark brow, hollow cheeks, and the anger, which, too, persisted throughout the months long isle of Samos experience, the island complex an inferno, the highlands of it in ruby descension. The demarcated flesh of nymph Theophane began to puce. The semi-highlands were vacant and they were tactile vulnerabilities. The responsibilities of nymph Theophane included the well-being of isles. Even more so, a common insult she wrought, the fury Poseidon hath, which stuck in her side like a blade of a knife was that she stole away to the lowlands in an attempt to flee. Once there, God Poseidon caught her and the debauchery did not end till Leo constellation was found in the sun, jammed and sultry. Asklepios fought off the heathen demoniacs. Really, he was baffled by the lust shown by Poseidon and was quite afraid. The God with his rod did well, the detached nymph Theophane charmed.

He was angered by this development in the yen of Poseidon for the uprisal threatening the Underworld and the unsure faiths of the Gods and of humans surrounding his rod, the true rod of healing, which Hermes, with desperateness, wanted to overcome with his own rod, a lesser rod and not as impressive, capable of healing, but in a remote sense; and the punctuality of the sacrifice of the golden ram, the appropriate nature of the usage of the Rod of Asklepios to heal nymph Theophane back to God form, and the citrine will of Apollo, whose ram was once his own, compelled the justification of such healing powers in the Rod of Asklepios and in the will of Asklepios into disparate quarters of divine solace, with basalt grins and with fervor. There was no denying the wisdom Asklepios wielded by his eyes and the look they gave his listeners, by way of captivity as that scint constellation. It had been the love of Hygeia which brought wrath on he.

Killed and resurrected, for the fear Zeus possessed in the knowledge of recent comprehension Asklepios assumed, how to resurrect the dead, led him to his original death. At the conclusion of his time as the constellation Ophiuchus and the hearty sufficiency felt by Zeus in his punishment dealt Asklepios for his, as was had, inappropriate knowledge of the Art of Resurrection, the reacquisition of the Rod of Asklepios was in question and the matter. The Rod of Asklepios, a single serpent entwined rod, was shadowed by the Rod of Hermes, which, with desperateness, wanted a cusp of maturity.

Nymph Theophane, almost killed by lust, began disgorging nebula and *astaria*, fluid tangents in geometry and Plantæ. Father and daughter, Asklepios and Hygeia watched the nymph descend into tonic psyche, convulsing and spastic. Spasmodic and contorted, the nymph Theophane was now, and in entirety, the responsibility of father and daughter, Asklepios and Hygeia, while Poseidon had her posterior. The bad conditions might always get worse for nymph Theophane if this cyclical, repetitive theatric ever went on much longer. It was for this motive the God of healing, Hygeia, with desperateness, wanted the *ayion*, Arthur Ioannou, to complete his sequence of code and begin feeding and clothing the impoverished peoples of the Earth. One year, the sacrifice of the golden ram could be obstructed and prevented by dumb Animalia or a slip up in the simulations of Hermes by the over-populated emotional cacheés on Mount Olympus. It were to be the day of the darkest reckoning. The uprisal in the Underworld were to take place. The damned souls of men were to walk upon Amaranth. A simplistic do not be was insufficient. The holes in the contemporary Mount Olympus were always noticeable and broadening. The code as written by the *ayion* may be that saving grace for Hygeia. The ability to reiterate the Art of Resurrection redoubled in Hygeia so that she may enact inspiration.

The means of such inspiration compartmentalized classical mythology into contemporary religion. The messages broadcasted themselves in the favor of the *ayion* Arthur Ioannou as Orthodox religion. It was a practice shunned by many Gods atop Mount Olympus, but Hygeia was rebellious and young. The westward facing Ezekiel, by the violent convulsions witnessed by Hygeia in the nymph Theophane, suggested the fury of the Testament was enough. All were affected by He. Whether the peculiar Gods knew it or not, Old Testament religion dictated their lives atop Olympus, thus the threat of war. It was a good reprehension she were of the warrior class of deities atop the Mountain, but the birth of temporal lobe epilepsy was scary and became more so a probability with the uprisal in the Underworld and even the succinctness of the code of the *ayion* Arthur Ioannou. The possibility of granting the *ayion* inspiration sequenced forlorn countenance and toxic relations. The nymph Theophane failed not, in her pithy contortions, to gain the sympathy of Hygeia, who took her kind countenance for an outward turn, at which point she spoke her name to nymph Theophane, who felt much of her incandescent favor. The God Poseidon finished.

The nymph Theophane, healed by the rod of Asklepios, awaited her revival. Same as the past years, the rod of the God Asklepios were to raze electric currents up her crippled spine. For a stretch of years, back in the original murder of Asklepios when he was the constellation Ophiuchus, the tribulations of nymph Theophane following the finish of Poseidon prolonged an already difficult healing process.

The Saccharum fields dwelt within spheres of less-than-virile pressures. The cane of sugar whitened the teeth of the impoverished farmers and strengthened them. Over the course of the year, during which nymph Theophane was on the island of Samos, the Saccharum fields bowed brown and flaked away under the heathen sun. Asklepios resurrected, nymph Theophane healed, the tall grasses of dental heartiness reinstilled their previous worthiness. A heady swoon took Asklepios as he escaped his prison, and he took as many specimens Chiroptera with him to the ochre fields of Saccharum to ward off the locusts, which buzzed throughout the hot season as naturalistic tambourines, the thumb of he, Apollo, runned up the sides of the instrument. To listen with nearness always betrayed a sense of young, lonesome solace. Thus, the Earth aged not.

Asklepios had, in his white eyes and exuberant bosom, grown wise past his years. The rod of healing were reassumed by he. His was one of true, holistic health, with the serpent and the olive branch. Vortex orations and gallant tables were held for the resurrected God Asklepios. Following his stint as constellation Ophiuchus, Gods and men alike chewed the Saccharum Plantæ and swallowed its thick nectar for taste and chewed its fibrous cane for hygienics. Atop Mount Olympus, amidst the incessant recoil of nymph Theophane on the island of Samos—she had not been released for the as of yet to be sacrificed golden ram—Asklepios stood and spoke atop the marble flooring in regards to his undeniable power through his rod of healing in the Art of Resurrection, a skill which he had kept by the good nature of God Zeus and through his talent for reticence ascertained while ensconced as the constellation Ophiuchus, which roiled and spat the cosmological Chiroptera of horror; nebulas of brilliant Aurora casted along his brow a brazen, indelible force not far separate from immortality, which made his reprehension stellar and worthy; Zeus forked lamb into his mouth and was forgiven; Hera spun in her dress; Hermes and Apollo plucked notes throughout the evening company; Hygeia sat aside, relieved that her father had been disgorged from the constellation Ophiuchus without harm and without lasting damage, or so she felt.

The recurrences of the, as she called them, bleak visions of swooning Chiroptera, their teeth, and their braying sonic-location persisted. Blind, Asklepios picked up, too, the ability to locate items, material and emotional, with sound. The constant smell of aphids, which shimmied up his nostrils, and the sly specimens Serpentes carried with him when he lay in his cotton bed, on Mount Olympus, at night. Each day, the God

Asklepios woke and the recollection by he of teeth entering the candescent epithelium tissue recast their horror within his pearl eyes, and he suffered much during his time not within but as the constellation, disparaged, disembodied, and punished for the mere possession of the knowledge, the Art of Resurrection, which had been granted him by Hygeia with such personable antiquity, amidst silken pillows, furled coverlets, and during heat, and with her woman parts, in secret, smelt by he, God Asklepios, who had been roused from sleep, and who was to be the receptor of such a gift as the Art of Resurrection, which he learned with rapidity as his daughter mounted and rode his stolid hard part. The morn, which followed, had Asklepios within the council chambers telling Zeus and Hermes of his irrefutable skills in the Art of Resurrection, and Zeus, who had grown fearful of its reiteration to the human race, an instance, or circumstance which was all too the case with the *ayion*, smited the God Asklepios for an eternity as the torturous constellation Ophiuchus, an act retrogradous and selfish, conceited and childish by he, Zeus, and the opportunity had presented itself for Hermes to take to retaliation for the strong and powerful words of God Asklepios that his rod of healing was the best and better than the rod of Hermes, who decided with quickness, to take to the home of the father of God Asklepios which was the home of Apollo and steal his herd of sheep and ram for jest and revenge. The insult undergone by Hermes was unlike any he had ever before. The relayed declaration, as rebuttal against that which were immediate, and that which were called superiority, and the declaration of God Asklepios that he knew how to resurrect man and God, hurt the innate relevance of Hermes and Zeus; and these antics were once more the matter with the *ayion* and his attempts to hack Hermes's simulations.

Hermes and Zeus consulted within the chambers of Hermes. "I have just spoken Hygeia into perhaps a held tongue. She, I think, very much so wants the *ayion* to succeed."

Zeus spoke in his Byzantine. The language came easy to him and he spoke it mad. "Hygiea is becoming dismissive. The youth in her blood is not a saving grace. She must know the code is a growing danger. How might she, with definitiveness—"

"Calm yourself."

"We must administer the Baucis and Philemon trial."

"Yes, my lord."

The fearfulness was unlike that of the great war. The war with the titans exhibited a fear that was ephemeral. A God might die, but the immortal celebration had them revive and live on as Gods. The Art of Resurrection, however, threatened their stocks of grain, barley, and wine, for overpopulation in the realm of the Gods which was Mount Olympus. It was this fear, which once more found itself in God Hermes and in Zeus. The code, on which was working the *ayion* rocked that world. The world was about to change. If Hermes did not stop him in the Cäerra hour, Shabbithai Mathon Neferition, the uprisal in the Underworld took grand place, men took to Gods in their beds, and favor did fast replete. To fortify the constancy, Hermes stole the gold herd of God Apollo, for retaliation but also for the luck of the supreme Gods and the fleeting symbol of truth, the val, golden fleece.

One week following the finish of the God Poseidon, the golden fleece was to hang from an oak tree in a grove within the Albigensian Peninsula. Coming from the coast along the Black Sea, Hermes looked and saw the golden fleece, and it was guarded by many mystical fauna and a spell, which aroused soldiers if the fauna were killed and buried. It had yet to be hanged there. It were in the original journey up the coast of the Black Sea for the original sacrifice of the golden ram when Hermes decided to create the barbito. Only the notes plucked by barbito masters made the Black Sea and its water higher. The golden fleece was of one head in the herd, which was stolen from Apollo; dire as the predicament may have been, Apollo was granted his barbito by Hermes, who kept the herd, but before returning with the instrument played a song for all sheep save one, the golden ram, and changed them all into white for his attire and his ritual simulations. The mythical barbito was played one time by Hermes to ward off hooves of brass, breath of fire, and toothy soldiers and to petrify the heads of sheep into wearable hides. The barbito—crimson shell, reeds, an ox hide, sheep belly strings—strummed the mild God of land travel and thievery over the fields of Saccharum.

Every village in Mesopotamia grew it. Saccharum, the tenth Century golden crop birthed mice. It brought instinct into the world; and who was to say when escape and when fight but one's own intuition, which took them away to their own imminent graveyards, where they did sleep within spectral visions of stark youth and wot health. Throughout the night, the fields of Saccharum zought Chiroptera. The swooned roosts, which came out nights, blotted out the hearty stars in impressive constellation Ophiuchus.

They gained true, sustained flight by batting hide wings. Hermes observed the swelled roosts of Chiroptera. An intruder was in his midst and God Hermes knew, with realization, the danger he was in and winced. Their leather wings grew white and then abated. Hermes murmured to himself then looked closer to find the bats one by one disappeared. The *ayion* was sure to write his blazing sequence. The Chiroptera blinked out of Earthy existence. Hermes screamed out. If this went on long all were to be Mortal Argonautica.

The halcyon ikons stood alit, with constancy. The church and its doors were open. Relief came. The husband and wife, however, locked lips beneath the large and enlarging mid-morning sun, with hair slicked back and coated with the salts of Earth. She licked his shoulder and stated she were thirsty for a beer. Children danced, nude, along the beaches of a near utopia. The tribulations of riots never had reached Greece's end. Telegraphed signals of painters like Monet and Rembrandt, Warhol and Dali danced in the stead of nix. Before the users, there were the oasitic Elysian rays. There, they had turned exit into virile ultra-nutrients. Absolution oscillated into the body and blood of the Mary program. Arthur dried his own body. He rubbed down Kaitlyn's sallow. The grapes and strawberries found their places in the pack. They had brought to the beach their blistering desires. Towards the café they tracked sand. They had been already guests in the café upon their first night in the town and did frequent the café. Mavrovouni placidity was then fast assumed. The order, an Irish cappuccino and a beer, were quickly consumed. Upon exit back onto the shore road, Arthur and Kaitlyn ran to the church.

The race, too, quickly digressed. The church stood on property just large enough for its quinine size. With a warm rush of air met, the waned-in-energy Arthur Ioannou examined close the Aurelian ikons on the walls. A gold-plated cup was seen on the white alter. Its largess bore the markings of archangels and saints. The westward facing mural of Ezekiel did patronize the nymph Theophane. A modern demarcation blotted out her hardships. The tribulations of the nymph remained ominous. They were not yet celebrated. Had the patron saint Ezekiel fought rather than smote, the trite foreboding of worship may have wrought the Cherubim and wheels of wagons. Aspects of the real *ayion*, noticed one after next, made the heads of lions. To walk Babylon and to tread the Earth, to access the incense scented church and to pull Yo'he'vah'he for the muse—mellow and elusive, O!—entranced the ace software engineer, Arthur Ioannou, when he lay down nights. Long battles with fatherhood, property, and volition, enriched his knowledge. For the civil disobedience he'd known, the causations of such war remained mythological and settled upon the petals of flora in patience of seismic and lien voidance. His shoulders had felt pressure. When the pew opened and the dust motes elevated, Gaap was assumed. Perhaps that was whiskey; but the morrow took them to Creté. There was dully noted optimism in that house. The priest said hello in Greek. "*Hygeiasas*." He was a round, pink man with long ears and a stout chin. Arthur sensed a reprehension in that priest. "*Hygeiasas*," said he once more, and the priest got his kiss on the hand.

Kaitlyn and her symmetrical face brightened at this gesture, and she laughed.

"You are Greek. My smart, innocent people, you must be Greek." The priest spoke broken English.

"I am searching for the words," said Kaitlyn. "I married into his kin."

"Kith and kin," said the overweight priest. "I've heard it. My blessed and innocent people, you are Greek."

"*Hygeiasas*," Arthur said. He said in attemptable Greek, "You have a very good church." Along the wall, the archaism eradicated the zeal from out of the temperate, phthalo Earth, but not until much later on.

They walked, not raced this time, far from their spot to where park swings hung suspended in between two titanium rods and swung side by side. Aphids peppered their faces. They grew starved and who by the cool, conditioned café did they meet outright. The mind of Arthur had grown quite keen by what dervish flood seemed to be not the sole one; the small, fried fish, which were called *marides*; spices; natural order of oceanic life; and fishermen and nets—all bloomed in dim lighting with common fate.

Arthur finished the plate of *marides* too well. A girl in a dark robe strode inside the café, whom he knew. It was the hot English girl. She had a glass in her hand. She then placed down the glass on the bar top. The bartender got her a vodka and cranberry. Arthur, Kaitlyn, and the English girl were all inside the abondant café. It was about eleven in that candescent morning and rising. Arthur did, with providence, bid the English girl sit. The brown-haired girl sipped vodka cranberry and then spoke.

The disingenuity was intelligible. English girl must have been mad. She drank down half her cold drink. "Brain freeze," English girl said. "Don't mind I'm sitting with you. I'm an open girl. I'm Bonny."

"It's no matter. You're more than welcome," Kaitlyn said. "To sit with us."

"I returned the glass Mark stole."

"Good for you," Arthur said.

"He's such a prick."

"Surely," Kaitlyn said. "There must be—"

"No," said English girl. She laughed, and she laughed hard. "No, it's meaningless." She finished her vodka cranberry and flagged down the bartender for another drink. "He asked me here from our place in Londie. I had just met him some three months prior our arrival in Greece. He's a prick. He's misogynistic. He's useless. He's stupid and fat. He's a wot, a scare."

Arthur said, "Dark robed mother: Do not be so exceedingly cast down."

"It's difficult. This is like a commune. What are these seemless people?—"

Kaitlyn said, "Where is he now?"

"He's washing himself in the ocean, love."

"I'm glad for that—"

The English girl said, "I think he was a prisoner, or criminal in his past life. He belongs in Aussie."

"You might be right," said Kaitlyn.

"We should have gone to Aussie,." said English girl. "And not bothered these peaceful people."

"Aussie," Arthur said, "is crazy." The software engineer was well aware of the disorder of a civil type, which went on in Australia, and found himself with suddenness quite interested in this conversation and in the English girl.

"Mark says Aussie is a prison."

"I wouldn't go so far." Arthur took down his Irish coffee all the way.

The bartender brought over the English girl's vodka cranberry. "It's an island prison he says and he aims to stay out of prisons. He wanted to stay on the mainland and we all did. Maybe he's superstitious."

Arthur ordered a whiskey straight. "That's an assumption."

"Mark takes to a religious psyche when he's confined. He gets crazy when there's even a bit of confinement. Can't stand it."

"That's human."

"The wignog is very easy going, though."

"That's enough."

"I can see myself on a faraway island," said Bonny. "Separated from the world, which weighs down my heart. I bid adieu," she said, and drank her vodka cranberry. "Wish me good luck with meek persons."

"Good luck with meek persons."

The English girl, Bonny, left twenty Euro on the café table and walked straight out of the small café. A salad for Arthur and Kaitlyn had then arrived. This was the last day Mavrovouni could afford them. It was a Friday afternoon, enough time for Arthur to make one more stop before leaving Mavrovouni for the city.

Arthur returned to the church just before sundown. He went and lit a candle. Those were the religious customs. Arthur entered the small nave. The priest chased the *ayion* in through the high narthex entrance. They sat in the stacidia and were quite silent. The manouelia crackled before the angel. The beautiful gates open, Arthur looked at the sanctuary seconds.

The priest spoke. "Will you come to liturgy Sunday?"

Arthur said, "No, we are leaving Saturday around one o'clock."

"That's all right," said the priest.

"I have a question for you I wish to discuss, please."

"It is my duty to listen as did the Herald."

"You speak good English."

"Thank you," said the priest. "I try in choice times."

"I appreciate your time."

The priest said, "No matter," and shifted in his seat.

"I spoke to somebody this afternoon who interested me quite much."

"Good, do tell more, my kind guest."

"She was an English girl and talked about a boyfriend," Arthur said. The templeton stood tall to he who had come to church. The horos and Pantocratores always vexed him. Their chimes and gold-plated décor did puzzle the software engineer, and he was very amazed. "She spoke and said her boyfriend does not like confinement. Said he can't stand it." All was quiet. "Do you like being here, Father, and feel uplifted by the spirit?"

"Of course, yes."

"So many people are poor. I aim to change that, Father."

"Dreams. Dreams can be quite childish. How can you possibly win the fight against darkness of such a degree?"

"I feel that is my duty, as is your own to listen. So, riddle me this father. In the Good book—I haven't read much of it—does disorder reign always, for ever and ever, until the day of Armageddon?

"Forgive me, I do not understand what you're saying," said the priest.

Arthur laughed, and then guffawed. "Is immorality to stay?"

"Goodness is Man's, naturally. I cannot hear a bit of arrogance in your voice. You have been unharmed for the entirety of your special life." The priest scratched his balding head. "But, there are a few things to watch out for, in God's eyes. Riches are one of them, sir."

Arthur said, "I do believe you, Father." Arthur said, "So, this English girl's boyfriend. She believed he was a criminal in a past life."

"No, I will not forget you," said the priest. "People come in here, tourists, and some people in families, the extended members of which I do not know well enough to feel, with confidence, that I will recall them. People come and people go. I try to recollect much. It seems the people of Earth move very fast now. What would happen if we were to remain very still?"

"We would be apt to starve," Arthur said, "and die. That's routine, Father."

"I try to stay very still. I am very much alive, but motionless, my friend."

"Warmth, food, science. All is good," said Arthur. "I aim to change from solitude to activity. We are going to Creté. I will work there on something. Perhaps, it will change the world."

The priest said, "What do you do for a job?"

Arthur said, "I am a software engineer. I work with computers for my health."

The priest hummed.

"Perhaps, I will work for the health of others, Father."

"Health is good."

"Health is very good, Father, but one needs money for health."

"Riches are one thing to be wary of, Kirio. What one needs for health is a football to play with friends." The priest said, "Stay in one place for a while. Stay for the liturgy and you will win your fight."

"I cannot, Father," Arthur said. "We have a schedule to keep."

"That's all right."

Arthur said, "I know you are right, Father."

"Perhaps, I have inspired you. But, if not, look at that fire you have close and know that God is watching you. Make good decisions. I will lead you from the narthex."

Arthur said nothing and walked through the Royal Doors and out through the opposite end of the narthex. He had come, by the priest, very convinced. Arthur walked back to the hotel and found Kaitlyn roused. Kaitlyn had been sound asleep. Arthur stroked her head with her tumultuous brown hair. He lay down and watched the flares until he did dream the infernal.

At noon, the drive to Athens commenced, without slain sheep. The herd by then was bygone. The hairpin turns of Peloponnesian roads zought fragrant pollens and beamed verdant. Heightened filaments of dust conducted opacity. The ferry ride took a day from Athens to Creté.

"Catherine," Arthur said. "Is meeting us there. She and I will link up our computers, and her boys will have fun with you. Visit a mountain or better yet an aviary."

"An aviary?"

"We have to get work done by ourselves if that's okay."

"That's okay. I will take them to visit a mountain or an aviary, Mr. Hitchcock."

"*The Birds* wasn't that scary."

"Bats are scarier than birds," Kaitlyn said.

"We'll have a Chirop- experience while in Creté."

"That's fitting." Kaitlyn was reading Stoker. They had had a conversation on bats, feeding specimens on the roof. Kaitlyn had come back and had jumped right back into *Dracula*. She was near finished with it.

Arthur said, "I have a feeling we will make progress on Mary."

"Good luck, Art."

"Luck has nothing to do with it, my soft and supple wife."

"That's how I like it, Arthur. Keep it up."

"Always, Kait."

Kaitlyn said, after a minute, "I want to talk to Allison before we embark."

"Yes, we can make that happen."

"It's been a month, with no speak."

"Why, I talked to her last week."

Kaitlyn said, "Not me. I feel rather bad."

Arthur said, "It's no problem. She's well, healthy, and matronly as always for the word." For a time, all matters were the Piræus-Heraklion ferry route. To drive into Athens heist sights of architecture, which took on two, and then three plus stories' determination. The metropolitan chaos presented itself, as two lines. Crossed by motorcars and Vespas, pedestrians and stray dogs, order was affray but to any other metropolises in the world dissimilar to quite an extensive degree. Athens had progressed much with its open-air markets and djembe players, the beggars and *tavli* patrons. That raillery joined Arthur's and Kaitlyn's own entering their apartment. The inscribed planter shape remained on the wall. The sandal was where they had left it upon their exit for Mavrovouni, on the countertop. The viridian tapestry of Cervidæ and nymph, too, remained immobile, nailed to the wall; the pein hammer, on the dining room table, suggested it get returned before their imminent trip to Creté. Arthur said, "I am going to the market to get some melons." He very much so adored his wife and had had the intention of getting her a jade necklace prior their departure back to the United States.

Kaitlyn said, "Get the cantaloupes, Arthur. The cantaloupes are so good. Where is the tablet so I can phone our Allison?"

"It's in the drawer in the night stand. Tell her I said hi."

"I will, Art." At that she strode into the master bedroom and changed. She came back out with the tablet in her hands, and she sat down at the couch and phoned Allison, their daughter, on the facetime application.

Arthur already wore shoes. They stayed on when he got into the house, in Athens. The chime of the application rang out, quiet. Allison answered the phone. Kaitlyn was quite elated, seeing her round, white face. She was a good-looking girl and took the round characters from her father. Her eyes and nose were Mother's. They talked about this coming year and Valentine's day.

"It's August," Kaitlyn said.

Arthur laughed and exited the apartment. The street uncurled, with its cars and chamomile scent, toward the open-air market. The market was a white Godsend. All were sold. Nothing was taken for chance. The gypsies begged for money and cast trodden looks. A multitude of faces, smooth and sun worn, walked and lined the market, which was laden with fruit and necklaces, instruments and pamphlets. Arthur picked up a cantaloupe and smelled its stem part. Another was risen by the complacent software engineer. The stem part was, deep, inhaled. He held them both chest high, with the stem parts outward; the good-looking stall keep laughed. Five euro were placed on the stall table top. The resplendent market faded rearward. Man walked home.

Often times, the effluence of youth came back in a breezy draft. It penetrated Arthur Ioannou as a reminder of his childhood health and rebelliousness. The man exuded an outward tranquil but he processed many kinks, with awkwardness. He might take a step too far in one direction and forthwith. It seemed what brought him to presence was the system of wind, which constantly assented his mind. It changed and redirected him, he, a lone monolith, shifted by the hands of guise. There, the road turned off onto his own. The short walk lasted two minutes before he got to the door. The front door, opened by Kaitlyn, read their address in large, yellow numbers. "I saw you from the balcony."

Arthur said, "Good and thanks for opening." The king bed ruminated.

"Oh, the cantaloupes smell good." Kaitlyn once more extruded her legs on the futon.

"The cantaloupes smell good. What is the matter, Kaitlyn?"

Kaitlyn sounded despondent. "I really miss Allison."

"We'll see her when we get back to the States, but for the next two weeks you and I will be in Creté, I'll get some real work done, and we'll buy her a bicycle when the big bonus comes in. How does that sound, Kaitlynmou?"

"It sounds really good, Arthur," said Kaitlyn. She lay on the overstuffed couch and began to cry. "Art, make the time go faster. A big, stinking bicycle doesn't make us better parents."

Arthur cut cantaloupes in the kitchen, with a knife.

"I am feeling so little," Kaitlyn said. She did sigh and did project some impatience for Greece. Neither was Kaitlyn a

Greek girl, which made her feel strange. "I feel small. Arthur, I feel small. Take me far away."

Arthur walked into the living room, with a plate of cantaloupe. "I will take Creté to you." He ate a cube of melon, then closed his lips around another and kept them both in his round cheeks. Kaitlyn laughed.

The day arrived when they went to Creté. Their bags packed, they boarded a train for the launch place of the Piræus-Heraklion ferry route. The scent of salty ocean was omnipresent. Gulls squaked above their heads, and there was not a shortage of the birds. In fact, there was a great abundance. So much so that Kaitlyn remarked at their numbers. The gulls circled around the quay. Arthur brought with them a cooler, for the lengthy trip, their suitcases, and his computer. He very much so looked forward to working with his associate, Catherine, on the Mary program, but tacit as he may have been about the subject the first budded currents of excitement entered his loins. The hefty machinery, a desktop computer, was stowed in an extra suitcase; and he looked forward to meeting Catherine's twins, too. Kaitlyn was to take them up Mount Ida, or Psiloritis, when the two software engineers worked on the shepherd program. With immediacy, the Mediterranean æsthetic roused the excitement in Arthur and Kaitlyn likewise, and they watched the dancers, who, on the quay, celebrated the fine weather. The husband and wife were young, just over the forty years of age mark, and felt younger in the incubator of a dock area. The ferry was in port. Its metal hull reflected the sunshine into the water and the water back at the hull of the ferry. It was an abundant place. Octopus was sold from a lament dockside kiosk. Youngest of children ran and toyed with one another; carefree atmospheric dropped. The ferry, which was to take Arthur and his lovely wife through the Piræus-Heraklion ferry route, blew its horn, because they were about to embark. The ship carved through the pearl sea. Creté was not too far off. It was ample worlds away.

Arthur said, "Do you want an ice cold beer?" The ferry launched in due time. The passengers were on their way to glaucous Creté. "I'll get you an ice cold beer."

"In five minutes I'll have one."

"Yes, of course."

The youthful and livable scents of the sea consumed the passengers and for Arthur Ioannou made the activation of motivation accessible. Arthur noticed the music had been turned off and was relieved. The swollen breakages of the Aegean Sea listened to words spoken as much so as the passengers listened to the crashes upon a metal hull, which blinked, candescent, in the forelight of another ascended, Greek mid-morning. It had begun to heat up. Over substantial crests and troughs, the ferry rose and fell into the bosom of the undulated Earth.

"If I could change one thing about you, Art, I wish you would dance more with me."

"I'm not much of a dancer."

Kaitlyn said, "I've seen you dance long ago. You were not so very bad. It was at your Uncle's wedding and you looked so pleased."

Arthur said, "I recall my Uncle's bride requested I dance. Fine, you want to dance let's dance, Kaitlyn, before we get there."

"Not here. There's so many people and we're on a boat."

At concessions, Arthur had a feeling he were right. It was best to loosen up. Such effects always unfolded positivity. The ferry still was close by the coast and fishing boats were within distance to see. The boats of fishermen, large and small, sailed adjacent the large ferry. A multitude of fish had already been caught this morning by professional fishermen, Arthur sighted, in the nets, which covered each of the close by fishing boats. *Marides* and fish of a larger type were detected by the software engineer, and he glinted at the notion Catherine, his associate, were to ride the Piræus-Heraklion ferry route with her twins next week, for the rendezvous. The ferry ship stayed course southward and sweltered in heat. It was the peak of summer. Denizenry were just taking to cooler atmospheres in their homes and avoided the outdoors as best as they could, for comfort. A cold beer was warranted.

Some odd hours later, the fatigue abated at the sight of the Cretė docks. The basin, oblong, rendered the entirety of the island in an unmistakable appeal. There was a certain magic in Cretė that made all which lived on the isle a sovereign instant of *agapi* to expire valiance cracked, because there were no goodbyes on the sere island, and if there were, the forces of Earth reconciled friction with more limelight inborne. The aqueduct withdrew its gates and let in the ship. The wicket, which lined the dock, was busy with trekkers. Five hundred kilometres Southward lay Alexandria. In between the isle, on which Arthur and Kaitlyn walked, and the city of Alexandria lay sunken, twelve-hundred-year-old limestone animal sarcophagi and stone idols, ships, coins, jewelry and hieroglyphic tablets, and the illustrious temple to the Amun-Gerub and statuary. Time enabled that decadence. The will of Man flooded the Anubian reach. Mot had doubtlessly slipped. If always they caught fish.

Arthur and Kaitlin Ioannou arrived at their hotel around seven-thirty. The couple of travelers presently walked into a hotel suite adorned with French molding, a dining room, a king-sized bed, and loft. Then, into the master bath one of the sojourns trod. Arthur dawdled in the master bedroom and turned on the overhead light, such prehense unforetold. All from the temple of Amun-Gerub to the bountiful island of Cretė were splayed to let sing O Heavenly Muse of certain devaste counter revolts and voided tundras blot from existence. Within the coordinate hard drive he set down were spliced oblivion. Kaitlyn had changed her clothes to silk. Both lay down. The fresh paint of the hotel suite peeled back into the exquisite darkness of the Heraklion Caves. Head room spate. Feathered people flocked about. The Aves populace proceeded, turning in accordance with rude signs. At every turn and at every movement the primordial bell rung struck. Delicate crystaline, the property of porcelain, and white spec fumed. Blanc and living bodies found showers in temple Ra. Walls roused, gone. A displaced psyche and leaden persona wrought all forthwith contained to basin. Ceilings of alabaster buckled upon good sight. Just past their lustre the master bed substantiated the Heraklion Caves centered within them as the Ivorian Island in the Sky the Mot attempted. Mot and their hollow feet stepped on ebony. Before the temperate garden, which lay inside the Heraklion Caves, the *agele* Cassiel hit them back, for he were so inclined. The granite Aves shattered and recoalesced, in simultaneity. As this woodsiness, the virile inspiration of the *ayion* Arthur underwent the push and pull of the divine protectors of science and those of the homes which were that of the Gods. One inquirable token—the unified disagreeance of the work of *ayion* Arthur and Hygeia—maintained its stagnant nature through the havoc figures were not able to relate. To leave in lieu of slumberousness the clear waking hours, the itinerary were abided to, the Heraklion Caves visited as sure as, back in that suite, geology, in fact, formed; the round number, which eluded the sequence of code in question, sat subtered, broadcasting fiberoptics, which jounced those rocky bounds into conception. The Navarre likes, by the fortuitous slate of the eternal Heraklion Caves, cut in half remonstrative indiscriminations.

The subterranean phonetics bound and recoiled. Endless consternation lent berth from its source, the Heraklion Caves, to drudged faults in an attempt to make amends. It seemed that clout force were never to be in the right. The disparaged countenances ranged from gaps in melody to solid escarpments, thorough interpretations of nature to death. Implorations of men and women nixed milieu. The uncanny ammunition of the Gods ticked off. So many extensions were made to quell the unease. The stratum gaped to save face. All lengths undergone solvated but the headstrong candor of the unexplainable to no avail. Albeit this replete certain pomposity the adversaries discontinued.

About the Author

Anders M. Svenning was born in New York. He started writing with seriousness at the age of nineteen and has now been published in many literary magazines throughout the United States and abroad. Some of the most recent include *The Furious Gazelle*, *The Bracelet Charm*, and *The Drunken Llama*. Anders M. Svenning has a Bachelor of Arts in English: Creative Writing from the University of South Florida in Tampa. He was inspired to begin writing in 2009 after reading *Sphere*, novel by Michael Crichton. As a matter of fact, the film *Sphere*, starring Dustin Hoffman, acted as inspiration before the novel had been read, and many great pieces of literature by Anders M. Svenning have become the result of such inspiration. Anders M. Svenning is the author of *50 States Poetry* (Pansophic Press), *Verdant Grounds, Subtle Boundaries* (Adelaide Books), *Otus in Betulaceæ* (Adelaide Books), *Occipital Circus & Other Stories Regarding Phrenology* (HellBound Books), and *Life After Schizophrenia* (Scarlet Leaf Publishing House). Anders M. Svenning lives in Palm City, Florida.

www.ingramcontent.com/pod-product-compliance
Lightning Source LLC
LaVergne TN
LVHW051013080826
845145LV00009B/2599

* 9 7 8 1 9 5 4 3 5 1 4 2 4 *